WEBSTERS' LEAP

WEBSTERS' LEAP

EILEEN DUNLOP

Holiday House/New York

Library of Congress Cataloging-in-Publication Data
Dunlop, Eileen.
Websters' leap / Eileen Dunlop.
p. cm.
Summary: Eleven-year-old Jill, estranged from her older brother
since their parents' divorce, finds their relationship renewed when
she shares a strange adventure with him back in sixteenth-century
Scotland.
ISBN 0-8234-1193-1
[1. Scotland—History—16th century—Juvenile fiction.
2. Scotland—History—16th century—Fiction. 3. Space and time—
Fiction. 4. Brothers and sisters—Fiction.] I. Title.
PZ7.D9214We 1994 95-2075 CIP
[Fic]—dc20 AC

For Hamish and Alison Dunlop

Contents

WEBSTERS'
LEAP

1

A Video Film

Jill was drying the dishes in the tiny kitchen of the caretaker's flat when suddenly she remembered a book she had once read. It began with a vivacious, curly-haired girl called Amanda Cameron travelling from London to spend the summer at an ancient Scottish castle. On a sunny July day she was reunited with her long-lost father and driven for miles through wild, wonderful countryside.

"Oh, look, Daddy! A deer!" she had squealed excitedly as a magnificent stag cleared the mountain track in one graceful bound. Her father, a strong, handsome type had said something like, "Yes, darling. There are lots of wonderful things for you to see."

At last the car had crested a moorland ridge and Amanda, by now gasping with excitement, had seen a castle rising serenely across a tranquil valley. As she gazed at its golden walls and fairy-tale turrets, she had a mysterious feeling that it was her real home.

Well, good for you, Amanda, thought Jill sourly, scowling through the narrow window at the surly sky. The only things she and Amanda Cameron had in common were that they came from London and had curly fair hair.

Although her destination too was a castle, Jill's journey had been very different from Amanda's. As she drove with her mother, in sulky silence, from her home in Ealing to Heathrow airport, a thunderstorm had been growling over London. It had followed Jill north. A sky like hot porridge spread over Glasgow, and when she eventually located her father in the crowded arrivals hall, all he could find to say was, "Sticky, isn't it?"

There were damp patches on his checked shirt and sweat was running down his cheeks into his brown beard. On the way to the car park, the conversation had been sparse.

"How are you?"

"Fine, thanks. What about you?"

"Can't grumble. Thanks."

Then there had been the long, embarrassing car ride to Gryffe, not over hills stippled with fern and crimson bell heather but through the dirtiest, most depressing landscape Jill had ever seen. Admittedly the derelict coal mines and shattered factory buildings did peter out at last, and the road rose to a ridge above a valley. But its greens were dingy under inky storm clouds and Jill's first glimpse of the castle, a grim, hollow-eyed ruin on a spur of rock beneath a dark hillside, confirmed her worst fear. Dad had gone off his head. No one in his right mind would choose to live in such an awful place.

Mr Weaver had been silent for almost an hour, driving with the grave concentration he gave to everything he did. Jill squinted at him sideways, wondering why on earth her parents insisted on this ritual exchange of children which no one enjoyed. She supposed it helped them cling to the pretense that they each had two children instead of one, which only proved how out of touch with reality they were. Jill was starting to work out how many days there were between now and her return home on the first of September when her father surprised her. Almost as if he had read her thoughts and wanted to reassure her, he began to talk.

As the car slid through a grey village and began to nose up a winding, wooded track towards the castle, Mr Weaver explained quietly how shocked he had been when he was made redundant at the library, and what astonishing good luck it had seemed when a friend had recommended him for the caretaker's job at Gryffe. He said that he and Tad were a hundred times happier than they had been in the city, and his shy voice grew warm as he told Jill about the beautiful painted ceiling in the castle's great chamber, and the garden he was restoring with plants that grew there four hundred years ago. He enthused about the wild creatures he had seen on the hill: deer, blue hares, kestrels, adders and barnacle geese.

"Tad and I have made a video film to show to visitors," he said, unable to keep his pride a secret. "A guide to the castle and the country round about. You can see it in the evening, if you like."

Jill didn't reply, because she was having jealous thoughts of her brother Tad, settling into her room in London, having a cool shower, getting ready to go out to a Chinese restaurant with Mum. But later, after she had unpacked in Tad's bedroom and eaten a supper of baked beans and fish fingers in the tiny kitchen under the castle's eaves, she remembered her father's offer.

"I'd like to see your film, Dad," she said. It wasn't true, but it was only half-past seven and Jill had completely run out of things to say. Another hour had to be got through before she could decently slope off to bed. "I'll wash up while you get things ready," she added.

Her father agreed, padding away eagerly into the sitting-room to find the cassette and switch on the television set.

"Tad did most of the shooting," he called back. "I think he fancies being a film director when he grows up."

Jill made a rude face and squirted detergent petulantly into the sink.

"Tad, Tad, Tad," she muttered under her breath.

The storm was long in coming, but even inside the castle's massive walls its approach was palpable. The heat in the low-roofed sitting-room was overpowering, and at intervals lightning whitened the roughly plastered walls.

It had been a long, exhausting day for Jill, and although she wasn't afraid, the thundery atmosphere affected her. As soon as she had finished washing up and settled herself comfortably in a corner of the sofa, she began to yawn. After five minutes she was longing to sleep, which was a pity because, in spite of her annoyance with Tad, she liked the way the film began.

Tad and his father had taken their camera out in spring, when there were still ribbons of snow on the hilltops and the green sward outside the castle gate was bright with daffodils. They had filmed each other. Jill saw red-haired Tad in a green waxed jacket and gumboots, standing in a racing mountain stream to mend a spindly wooden bridge. She saw her father wearing tweed breeches and a brown waistcoat, digging in his garden. There were wonderful shots of boxing hares, a black-and-white snake curled up asleep on a bed of withered leaves, a clump of primroses opening in a patch of snow.

Then the camera moved indoors. Jill heard Tad's familiar voice drawing attention to the spiral staircase, the carved fireplace in the great hall, the painted ceiling in the room prepared for a visit of Mary, Queen of Scots to Gryffe in 1563. At the mention of this name Jill groaned inwardly.

Last summer, when she had stayed with her father in Edinburgh, he had insisted on taking her sight-seeing. One sweltering afternoon he had dragged her to the Palace of Holyrood House, and she had had to spend two hours trotting through its highly-polished rooms, staring glumly at ancient portraits, tapestries and furniture. The worst bit had been listening to Dad banging on about Mary, queen of Scotland at seven days old and widow of a French king at eighteen. Mr Weaver had obviously been crazy about her, and had spared Jill nothing of the marriages, murders and plots which had whirled her towards imprisonment in England and eventual loss of her head. Jill, who had no interest in the past, had been glassy-eyed with boredom, and now here was the wretched woman turning up again at Gryffe.

Before Jill had time to fret, however, sleep overcame her. While her father goggled in admiration at a film he must already have seen dozens of times, she dozed against a cushion. Thunder like a roll of drums aroused her. Her startled eyes were drawn back to the bright rectangle of the television screen and she had the weirdest experience imaginable.

Tad's voice had faded, and in its place was music, played on an instrument that sounded to Jill rather like a guitar. She knew the tune, and began to put words to it inside her head.

Lully lulla, thou little tiny child,
By, by, lully lullay.

It was called the Coventry carol, and she had learned it at school one Christmas. But as she stared at the picture, the rest of it floated out of her mind.

Jill was looking down a stone passage, arched like a

long, thin cave. In the doorway at the end of it stood a
girl and a boy, in what she supposed must be fancy dress.
The girl was wearing a grey gown with narrow sleeves and
a stiff, cone-shaped skirt down to her ankles. On her head
was a white cap, bulging where her hair was tucked up
inside it. The boy wore a fawn tunic with a white ruff at
the neck, long brown stockings and clumsy leather shoes.

They were too far away for Jill to see their faces, and
for a moment she watched them whispering, wondering
vaguely whether they were going to a party, or acting in
a play. She was caught off guard when suddenly they
turned and tumbled down the passage—towards the camera, of course, but to Jill it seemed that they were hur-
rying towards her. The boy came first, and with a spurt of
indignation she saw Tad's green-eyed, freckled face grinning under a flat tweed bonnet.

Showing off as usual, thought Jill crossly, and opened
her mouth to snap, "What an idiot!"

But another peal of thunder interrupted her, and by
the time the noise had died away she was too taken aback
to say anything. For Tad had passed behind the camera
and his companion's face, also smiling, filled the screen.
Jill only saw it for an instant, but it was like looking into
a mirror. The face was her own.

2

Tad's Room

Jill had scarcely been able to keep her eyes open all evening, but as she got ready for bed she felt wide awake again. She was the kind of person who liked reasonable explanations, so now she was doing her best to find one.

As she cleaned her teeth in the bleak white bathroom which was about the size of the airing cupboard at home, she tried out the theory that the lightning was to blame. Suppose it had caused an electrical fault in the television, which in turn had produced a freak image? This sounded weak even to Jill, who wasn't scientific, though slightly more credible than her next notion, that Tad had used a photograph of her to play a trick.

She also had to dismiss one or two other ideas as farfetched, and by the time she was back in Tad's little tower room, brushing the tangles out of her hair, she was already falling back on the most conventional possibility. She must have been dreaming. She had been asleep, and had only imagined she had woken up. After all, she did know the Coventry carol, and as for the strange clothes— well, dreams were dreams. They didn't have to make sense.

Jill was smoothing moisturiser onto her face when the storm finally broke. For the last ten minutes there had hardly been time to blink between lightning flash and thunder peal. Now the rain came, the first warm splashes thickening quickly into a deluge. Suddenly it was pelting down over the worn grey battlements, hammering on the slates, overflowing gutters and shooting through the gaping mouths of stone dragons at the corners of the roof.

Excited by the uproar, Jill jumped up in her nightie onto the wide stone sill and watched a silver cascade passing the window, bouncing off the courtyard far below. The sky was wiped out and it was almost dark, but through the wet glass her eye was caught by a movement.

Peering curiously, Jill saw a figure sheltering under a ruined archway opposite. Before she could really focus on it, however, it had whipped a dark cape over its head. Holding the cape like outstretched wings it sprinted across the streaming cobbles towards the castle. Jill tutted with exasperation. Honestly, she thought, what an ass Dad is. Imagine sitting around all evening, then remembering he had something to do outside after it had started raining cats and dogs. He must have come upstairs like the wind, though, because only a few seconds later she heard him close the door of his room, which was next to hers.

Gradually the storm diminished. At last the rain stopped and the thunder exhausted itself among the hills. Through the tiny window Jill saw the sky clear and a segment of moon appear behind the grid of panes. The silence after the tumult was absolute. Jill, who was only aware of the comforting hum of city life in its absence, felt—not afraid, because whatever the rest of the castle was like this little flat wasn't scary—but small, and missing Mum. Far away in the valley she heard the faint, precise sound of a church clock striking ten. It was all so unlike what she was used to that she didn't think she would ever get to sleep.

Curled up under the blue duvet, Jill looked around the moonlit room. Her eyes rested briefly on Tad's crammed bookshelves, his cassette rack, the tidy desk with his computer and printer and mugs of pencils and pens. On the white walls were posters from the Science Museum. Although it was about a quarter of the size of the room Tad had occupied when he and Dad lived in Edinburgh, it contained exactly the same things. There was only one difference. Before last year's exchange, Jill remembered with a little twinge of hurt, Tad had stuck notices all round the room saying: "Don't touch this" or "Keep out!" This year there were none. Jill wondered whether he was feeling kinder, or just reckoned that he had made his point.

Jill squirmed over on the unfamiliar mattress, pulled

the duvet over her head and tried to think about nothing. Only of course, that was impossible. The strange dream she had had earlier in the evening wouldn't be banished, and Jill recalled vividly the intimate, whispering figures and laughing faces of Tad and herself. The most fantastical thing of all, she thought bitterly, was that she and Tad had been having fun together, actually behaving like friends. The time when that might really have happened was now far away.

As always, thinking about Tad triggered in Jill's mind a replay of everything that had happened since the spring morning, four years ago, when she had gone with her parents and Tad to the Law Courts in London. There the judge who was dealing with Mum and Dad's divorce had taken her into his room, and asked her whether she wanted to live with Mum, or with Dad.

He was a nice old man who had taken off his wig and gown so as not to scare her, and when Jill, who was only seven, had said she wanted to live with both of them, had looked really upset. Gently he had explained that since Mum and Dad had decided not to live together anymore, that wasn't possible. It was his job, he said, to decide who would look after Tad and Jill. It would help him if he knew what Jill herself would prefer.

"What does Tad say?" Jill had wanted to know, but the judge had replied that he couldn't tell her that.

"It's what you want that matters, Jill," he had said, adding that of course she would be able to see the parent she didn't live with at weekends.

So Jill had thought quickly, and decided that it would be sensible to choose Mum. Her only reason was that Mum was a better cook than Dad. If she stayed with Mum, she would have nice things to eat during the week, and at weekends Dad could take her to McDonald's, which he often did anyway. It didn't occur to her that Tad, who enjoyed eating, might not make the same choice, and she would never forget the shock of learning that he had told the judge he wanted to stay with Dad. Worse still, the judge had decided to give them what they said they preferred. Jill was to live with her mother and Tad with his father, and both parents were to have what was called "access" to their other child.

For a while, although Jill had missed having Tad around at home, the arrangement had worked well enough. Every Saturday Jill went to Dad's flat, and usually to lunch at McDonald's. Every Sunday Tad came to Mum's house for the day. Weekends became special. Tad never came without bringing Jill a small present, and she had gone on thinking her big brother the most wonderful person in the world.

Then, almost two years ago, the unthinkable had happened. Dad, who had never really liked London, had suddenly announced that he was going to live in Scotland. He had been brought up there and always called it "back home." He had applied for a job at the National Library in Edinburgh and in a matter of weeks was gone, taking Tad with him. Jill had been angry with Dad, but it was Tad's pleasure she couldn't forgive. While she had cried in bed night after night, her brother had gone off to Edinburgh grinning from ear to ear.

To be fair, which Jill wasn't, Tad had telephoned, written letters and sent picture postcards. Parcels had arrived containing Jill's favourite chocolate fudge and a dry, gingery candy called Edinburgh rock. It was Jill who refused to speak to him, or write back, or eat his sweets. After a while Tad had stopped trying to keep in touch, and when they had all met in York at Christmas for a "family weekend," he and Jill had stared at each other like strangers. Indeed the atmosphere had been so hostile that their parents, agreeing for once about something, had vowed never to have such a get-together again.

Instead they hit on the idea of exchanging children during the summer holidays. They said quite openly that the main attraction of this plan was that it would keep Tad and Jill apart until they were old enough to be more sensible. It didn't seem to cross their minds that to make children live for seven weeks with each other's possessions, but without each other, was cruel.

Jill couldn't help crying a little. When she put her head out from under the duvet the moon had gone up the sky and Tad's room was in darkness. She heard the distant clock strike eleven, and not long afterwards sleep at last began to blur the sad pictures in her mind.

3

Sunday Morning

The next day, Sunday, began with burnt toast and another puzzle. Jill smelt the toast the moment she opened her bedroom door, and went along the passage to the kitchen wrinkling her small nose in disgust. She wasn't surprised to find a lump of margarine, a jar of instant coffee and a rack of blackened slices on the worktop. This, after all, was why she had decided to stay with Mum. She also found a note saying, "Gone for papers. Help yourself."

Thanks a bunch, thought Jill. With a sigh she tipped the toast into the waste-bin, found the loaf, heated the grill and made some more. Then she made herself a mug of coffee and took her breakfast to the little pine table by the window.

The flat was like an eagle's nest, dizzyingly high above

dense green treetops, and the view from the kitchen window was amazing. Far below Jill could see the roofs of the village in the valley, and hear the bell in the clock tower lugubriously calling people to church. The sky looked newly washed and the morning sun was drawing up curls of vapour from the damp fields. It was an Amanda Cameron morning, Jill decided, though it was hard to imagine Amanda sitting down in a poky kitchen to a breakfast of toast and margarine. Amanda's father had been terribly rich.

Jill had finished her toast and was drinking her coffee when her father appeared, carrying a thick bundle of newspapers and a carton of milk.

"Everything OK?" he asked, as he put the milk into the 'fridge and spooned some coffee into a mug for himself.

Jill nodded.

"Nice view," she said, then wished she hadn't when she saw how pleased he looked.

"Great," he agreed. "Better weather, too."

This was how they had been conversing ever since they met, in taut phrases which punctuated the silence without disguising their uneasiness with each other. Jill was finding it a strain already. There was a pause while Mr Weaver stirred hot water into his coffee and sat down with it at the table. Then Jill, aware that it was her turn to say something, asked, "Did you get soaked last night?"

There was no immediate answer. Jill saw her father's

dark eyebrows lift and his forehead wrinkle. Obviously he hadn't a clue what she meant.

"Soaked?" he repeated eventually. "Why would I be soaked?"

It was Jill's turn to look baffled.

"I thought—that is, I saw you," she said, recalling the bat-like figure she had watched loping across the courtyard. "From the window in Tad's room. In the rain, with a cloak over your head."

She willed him to remember too, but Mr Weaver only smiled vaguely.

"I wasn't out last night. You must have been dreaming," he said, unfolding the *Sunday Times*.

But Jill wasn't prepared to let the matter drop so easily. She had just managed to convince herself that she had dreamt herself on the video film, but she was sure she had been wide awake on the window sill, watching the storm.

"Does anyone else live here?" she asked urgently. "Dad, listen a minute. Could I have seen someone else?"

Mr Weaver had disappeared behind the newspaper, but his answer was firm enough.

"No, you couldn't. Our nearest neighbours are the Bowdens at Simpleside Farm, about half a mile down the glen. Which reminds me," he added, briefly poking out his nose. "Mrs Bowden will be coming up this afternoon. We open to visitors at two o'clock on Sundays, and she helps me in the shop."

Jill rinsed her mug and plate at the sink; then, since she didn't want to read the papers, decided to go for a walk. Suddenly she wanted to be out of doors.

As she descended the narrow spiral stair, however, Jill couldn't resist pausing to peep through the tiny arched doorways that opened from it. On each floor she saw a cold, stone-flagged room without furniture or glass in the windows. Perhaps Gryffe wasn't, as she had first thought, a complete ruin, but it was very close. There was a damp, earthy smell, and not until she was at ground level did Jill find a room with signs of modern occupation.

In a gloomy, vaulted apartment, wooden benches were set out in front of a large white canvas screen. Behind the benches a film projector and a video recorder stood on a shelf. There was no window, but when Jill flicked a switch four spotlights beamed onto the display of maps and photographs on the walls. Tad's work again, Jill supposed grumpily. Switching off the light, she hurried out into the sunshine. The first thing she saw was the tumbledown archway from which a dark figure had last night emerged in the rain.

Leaving the castle by the main gate, Jill walked pensively down the slope to the bridge which Tad had been mending in the film. Beyond it an earthy track wound up onto the hillside. Jill climbed with a chattering stream on her right, and on her left a spindly oakwood which thinned out like receding hair towards the tree line further up the hill. She was out of breath by the time she reached a little platform of turf beside a green pool, and sat down with her back to a rock. The valley shimmered softly, a plaid of green and violet under the high sun. It was beautiful, but by now Jill was too perplexed to notice.

She was tempted, of course, to agree with her father. It made good sense that last night she had been tired, the thunderstorm had made her dopey, and she had either dreamt or imagined strange things. The trouble was that she didn't believe it. She had certainly been wide awake as she got ready for bed, and had heard eleven strike before she fell asleep. So why on earth should she have been asleep on the window sill? And—here was a question that couldn't be avoided—if she was sure that she had been awake then, why should she assume that she'd been asleep when she saw herself on the television screen? She certainly hadn't thought so at the time.

The church clock in the village chimed noon, and as she counted the strokes an intense wave of homesickness washed over Jill. If she were at home she would have been to church with Mum, and now she would be down at the tennis club wondering what was for Sunday lunch. Instead of sitting alone on this alien hillside, worrying about things that couldn't be explained.

Blinking away tears, Jill glared down at Castle Gryffe, poking up its sharp slated roof through a froth of summer leaves. Unexpectedly a tiny figure appeared on the battlements, and a moment later the blue-and-white flag of Scotland broke from the flagpole.

Dad getting ready for his visitors, thought Jill—and in

a flash realised how silly she had been. For of course there was a perfectly simple way of finding out whether she had really appeared in the film. She only had to watch it again. She didn't even have to ask Dad to let her see it. It would be shown that afternoon for visitors, in the room with the canvas screen.

4

I Was There Too

By two o'clock cars were rocking slowly up the road and reversing into the car park at the end of the castle drive. From the sitting-room window Jill watched families spilling out of them, joining a trickle of young people, in colourful T-shirts and shorts, who had climbed up the glen from the village. A woman in a flowery dress, who must be Mrs Bowden, went into the little hut where tickets and guide books were on sale. Jill thought she wouldn't mind selling tickets. It would pass the time when she had nothing else to do.

Only right now, she reminded herself firmly, she did have something else to do. Coming back from her walk she had spotted a notice inviting visitors to watch "Around Castle Gryffe" in the ground floor chamber at 2:15, and although she had butterflies in her tummy, Jill was determined to be there. This time, she assured herself, she would be awake from beginning to end.

At ten past two she ran downstairs. In the ground floor room the lights were on and the visitors, already looking weary, were relaxing on the benches. Jill slipped in at the end of the back row.

"Isn't it a lovely day?" said a white-haired woman with a friendly face. "And where do you come from, dearie?"

"Ealing. That's in London," Jill told her.

"London? My, that's a far place," was the surprised reply.

That was how it seemed to Jill too, as she turned to watch her father putting a video cassette into the machine. Suspense was making her fidgety and she was thankful when he closed the door and switched off the lights. The screen was illuminated by the first frame—Castle Gryffe with daffodils.

Once again, despite her anxiety, Jill loved the tender pictures of flowers and animals, and the lilting Scottish tunes that accompanied them. She couldn't help being interested when she saw the pool she had visited earlier, and joined in the audience's gasp of horror when the camera showed the stream, which was called the Clathy burn, being sucked into a chasm between two jagged black rocks. Above the booming of the torrent Tad's voice announced that through this sinister gap, called Websters' Leap, the water fell forty metres into Rollo's Well below.

Just as before, however, Jill thought Tad's enthusiasm

for the castle plain stupid. She couldn't understand why anyone should be excited by a gloomy old building, and it depressed her to know that the family Tad seemed so keen on, the Romanes, were all dead—wiped out long ago by warfare, murder and disease. Portraits of them appeared on the screen, their pale, dark-eyed faces rising from ruffs, lace collars and cravats. They all looked alike, and the only one Jill remembered afterwards was a young woman holding a baby, a funny little creature stiffly dressed in a lacy frock and a white bonnet. Then there was Mary, Queen of Scots again, slit-eyed and watchful in a dark jewelled dress.

It wasn't Jill's scene. But this time she kept her eyes and ears open, and when the warning notes of the Coventry carol replaced Tad's voice she pinched her leg to make doubly sure that she was really awake. With a thrill that was half satisfaction and half apprehension she saw what she had seen before.

At the end of the long passage which, Jill suddenly realised, was the one between the kitchen and Tad's bedroom in her father's flat, the two oddly dressed, whispering figures again appeared. This time she knew the boy was Tad, and the girl . . . Oh, but surely, Jill thought desperately, she must have been mistaken. Never in all their lives had she and Tad stood together in that place. Whoever the girl was, she just couldn't be Jill. All the same, her chest was tight as she waited for the children to move, and her tongue hurt as it pressed against the dry roof of her mouth.

"Oh, hurry up," she whispered, and as if they had heard the two figures turned and ran towards her. First Tad—then herself. As the words The End appeared on the screen, Jill shivered violently in the stuffy room.

It was such a frightening moment that she wouldn't have believed anything worse could happen. But it could, and did. Mr Weaver switched on the lights, and before anyone could move he was making a little speech.

"Ladies and gentlemen, thank you for your attention. I hope you enjoyed the film. It may interest you to know that it was largely shot by my thirteen-year-old son Tad, who also wrote and spoke the commentary. He's away on holiday at the moment, but you saw him in the last sequence. He had the clothes for a school play about Mary, Queen of Scots, and I filmed him wearing them for a bit of sixteenth-century atmosphere." Mr Weaver grinned as he added, "Having heard Tad's voice, you won't be surprised to learn that in the play he was page to the English ambassador." He paused to give the audience time to laugh politely, then concluded, "I'll be around if you want to ask questions. Enjoy your afternoon at Gryffe."

Someone opened the door, letting in a draught of fresh air. The audience began to drift out into the courtyard, but Jill sat still, stiff with hurt and disbelief. Well, damn that, she thought. My son Tad. What about my daughter Jill? Tears rose in her eyes and she wanted to run to her father, shake his arm and shout, "What about me, Dad? Didn't you even notice? I was there too."

Only before she could move, a new and chilling possibility came into her mind. Her father had asked for questions, and she suddenly wanted to ask one, but it was so bizarre that she couldn't bring herself to ask him. Yet she had to ask somebody. Leaving Mr Weaver rewinding his film, Jill stumbled in the wake of the last visitors into the sunlit courtyard. Momentarily she was blinded by the brightness, but as her vision adjusted she saw the friendly old lady, standing in the archway to admire the view. Jill hurried over to her.

"Please, may I ask you something?" she asked, struggling to keep calm.

The old lady looked at her with some surprise, but nodded agreeably.

"Of course, my dear."

Jill swallowed.

"Well, can you tell me—at the end of the film we just saw, where Tad was dressed up—how many children did you see?"

The old lady looked even more surprised, but she answered without hesitation.

"Oh, just the one. Tad, if Tad is his name."

5

Loneliness

Unable to face the rest of the afternoon watching families enjoying a normal Sunday outing, Jill fetched her purse and stamped off down the long, stony track to Gryffe village. A general store was open on the main street; Jill bought cornflakes, orange juice, a jar of marmalade and a couple of magazines. The ordinariness of the street, with its sunburnt holidaymakers and children eating ice cream, did her some good. Her nerves steadied, and as she toiled back uphill with her shopping she took a decision. Like it or not, she would have to question her father.

There was just a chance, after all, that she had got it all wrong, and was worrying about nothing. The ground floor chamber had been stuffy, and the old lady might have been dozing on the bench. Dad might laugh and say, "The girl with Tad? She's Mrs Bowden's daughter, and come to think of it, she looks a bit like you." And if he didn't, Jill was sure she would know from the look in his eyes whether he secretly knew there was something strange about Castle Gryffe.

This resolution helped her through the rest of the day, which she spent reading her magazines on a bench in the walled garden. In the evening, however, when the visitors had gone home and she was in the kitchen laying the table for supper, Jill still found it impossible to blurt out her question. The prospect of being thought batty was so embarrassing.

Eventually she said, "Dad, does Tad have friends here?" thinking that she might find her way from this to what she really wanted to know.

Her father, who was cooking the sort of greasy fry-up her mother called "death by cholesterol," nodded vaguely.

"Yes, I think so. Other boys at school," he replied, cracking an egg on the side of the pan.

"Girls?"

"I suppose so. It's a co-educational school."

"Do any of them ever come here?"

Mr Weaver shook his head.

"We're very isolated," he explained, "and the high school's twelve miles away. Tad goes on the bus at eight o'clock, and he doesn't get home till after five. Weekends, we're busy with visitors." He flipped a slice of fried bread over in the sizzling fat and added rather defensively, "Tad doesn't mind being on his own at Gryffe. He has lots of things to do."

Jill, who remembered Tad as someone who always went around laughing with a crowd of mates, was tempted to say, "He must have changed." But she didn't want to antagonise her father, so instead she said carefully, "OK. I just thought—when you were making the film, you know—it might've been fun for Tad's friends to be in it too." She was ready to add, "Silly me! I forgot about her," if he reminded her that Tad had had a companion.

But there was no need.

"Funny you should mention that," Mr Weaver said. "Tad did ask one of the girls in the play to come here and be filmed wearing her dress, but she got flu and couldn't make it." He took the pan off the stove and emptied half the contents onto the plate for Jill. "Pity you weren't here," he added teasingly. "You'd look cute in a ruff and a little lace bonnet."

Fortunately just then the toast went on fire, so Jill didn't have to reply. But she had found out what she wanted to know. Her appearance in the film hadn't been visible to anyone but herself.

The next couple of days weren't at all enjoyable. Jill mooched about the flat or sunbathed in the garden, homesick and fighting off panic attacks. Her father's failure to see her on the screen disturbed her even more than having seen herself, and his cool dismissal of the notion that she might really have seen someone in the courtyard on the night of the storm was far from reassuring. Since she was certain that she had seen someone, it only gave her something else to worry about.

It was a measure of her anxiety and loneliness that she wondered briefly whether she should write to Tad, but she decided that she couldn't possibly take such a risk. Even if he did know something odd was happening at Gryffe, he might not choose to tell her. If he didn't know he would think she was absurd, and being laughed at by Tad was the most humiliating thing Jill could think of. Tad was often in her mind, however, and on Tuesday morning she had news of him.

"Letters from Ealing," said Mr Weaver, coming into the kitchen while Jill was finishing her breakfast. "One for you from Mum, and one from Tad for me."

If he had hoped that Jill might show interest in Tad's letter, he was disappointed.

"Thanks," she said, gulping down the last of her coffee, and took Mum's away to her room to read.

Jill had spoken to her mother a couple of times on the telephone, but with Mr Weaver within earshot at Gryffe and Tad, presumably, within earshot in Ealing, their conversation had been general. A letter was more intimate, and Jill opened the envelope with pleasurable anticipation. She wasn't disappointed.

The letter began with a few remarks about the weather, the cat and a burglary at number thirty-seven. Then the subject changed abruptly to Tad. Tad, apparently, was giving trouble. He wouldn't eat his brown rice and organic vegetables, he had sneered at the nice Bermuda shorts Mum had bought for him, and worst of all he had mortally offended Justin by asking if he was wearing a wig. Jill couldn't help giggling at this. She wasn't keen on Mum's boyfriend either. Justin put mousse on his hair and wore clothes like men in fashion magazines. The reek of his cologne spray was disgusting and Jill reckoned he was the biggest prat in Ealing.

"Remember I said I might take Tad to Cornwall for a week?" Mrs Weaver, or Ms Chancellor as she now preferred to be called, had written. "Well, I've changed my mind. He doesn't want to go anywhere—won't even get off his behind to feed Pussums. He sits in his room practising Christmas carols on an old lute your father bought for him—yes, Christmas carols, in July! I think if I hear that Coventry carol one more time I'll go loopy. Oh, and he says he's writing a book. I said he could use your computer. Hope you don't mind."

Jill did mind, but she was distracted by the coincidence that Tad too was thinking about the Coventry carol. And Mum's parting shot got her giggling again.

"If you ask me, Tad should never have gone to live in Scotland. He calls potatoes 'tatties,' and he's beginning to roll his Rs like your father."

Jill was still laughing as she went downstairs to the garden, but as she lay on the travelling rug in the sun she couldn't help thinking what a lonely life Tad seemed to lead. She was herself lonely now, but at least she knew that in September she would be home, playing with her best friend Benazir and riding her bike after school with the other kids in Lessington Avenue. There would be Guides to look forward to, and hockey on Saturday mornings.

Tad, on the other hand, now solitary in Ealing, would be just as lonely when he came back to Gryffe, with no friends to mess about with in the evenings and at weekends. No wonder he'd got interested in such crazy things. Making films, playing the lute, writing a book, for heaven's sake. For an unguarded moment Jill felt really sorry for Tad, and had to remind herself sternly that everything that had happened to him was his own fault.

6

Press "Enter"

For a few days nothing out of the ordinary happened, and although Jill certainly didn't forget the strange experiences of her first hours at Gryffe, she did begin to hope that they wouldn't recur. Her tummy stopped churning, and she was less often on the verge of tears. The good weather continued, with cool grey mornings melting into golden afternoons. Soon tiring of inactivity, Jill went exploring. One day she climbed Gryffe hill and had a view of distant blue mountains. On another she descended into the mossy, leaf-dark glen.

At first Jill felt adventurous, but before long she was rather regretting her expedition. The narrow paths were slippy, and rickety wooden bridges swayed above terrible clefts in the sides of the gorge. Jill felt dizzy, especially when she looked up at the gap where the Clathy burn overshot the rock. The bride's veil of tumbling water was beautiful but overwhelming, and Jill was glad to find a path leading from the trees into the sunshine. I shan't go there again, she vowed as she walked home up the main track.

Instead she began to help her father in the garden. This was a lovely place with billows of lavender, hollyhocks and pale pink roses, a gentle contrast to the gaunt, cold-eyed castle rearing above. Jill weeded the herb beds and dead-headed the roses, feeling peaceful for the first time at Gryffe.

Only when nagged by her father did she explore indoors. The castle didn't exactly frighten her, but she found its labyrinth of narrow passages and grey rooms depressing. The carved fireplace Tad admired so much seemed to Jill only a cold, empty hearth, and even new windows and a display of weapons in the great hall failed to alter its forsaken atmosphere. Only the painted ceiling in "Queen Mary's chamber" delighted Jill, and she lay on the floor for ages enjoying its suns and moons and jolly angels playing musical instruments. She was reminded of another Christmas carol:

> *There angels sing in jubilant ring,*
> *With dulcimers and lutes,*
> *And harps and cymbals, trumpets, pipes,*
> *And gentle soothing flutes.*

Although Jill still pretended to be deaf whenever her father mentioned Mary, Queen of Scots, she couldn't help wondering if she had loved the ceiling too.

Then the rain came. Overnight on Monday a carpet of cloud unrolled itself from the west, and when Jill woke at half-past seven on Tuesday morning the little room was almost in darkness. From the bathroom window she looked out over trees silvered with pinhead rain. An impatient wind was stirring in the branches, and during breakfast it rose suddenly. The drizzle thickened to a downpour and mousy mist wiped out the view.

"Is the weather often like this?" asked Jill fretfully, as rain hit the window like shrapnel.

"Yes," replied her father discouragingly. He licked marmalade off his fingers and added cheerfully, "A day in the office for me, I guess. What about you?"

"I haven't a clue," snapped Jill.

Mr Weaver didn't make any suggestions. He rose from the table and wandered off down the passage. Jill knew she wouldn't see him again until lunch time. This was what she dreaded most, a day cooped up indoors, surrounded by other people's possessions and with nothing she really wanted to do. Disconsolately she cleared away the breakfast things, then she too drifted down the passage to her room. She had remembered that there was a crossword competition in one of her magazines, and thought she might have a go. The prize was a trip to Disneyland, which would be a nice change from Gryffe.

No sooner had she shut the door, however, than the restlessness of a prisoner gripped Jill. She couldn't concentrate on the puzzle and soon she was prowling around, examining Tad's collection of fossils, looking at his bookshelves. Normally she liked reading, and Tad had lots of interesting books. But just now she didn't see a single one she wanted to read.

Jill's eye fell next on Tad's computer. It was the same as the one she had at home; both had been Christmas presents from Dad. Jill only used hers occasionally to play games, and it occurred to her that since Tad was using hers, she might use his to play one now. She switched the computer on and began to rake through drawers and cupboards, searching for a suitable game. Only Tad didn't have any games. She might have known.

In the desk drawer, however, there was a single disc in a little cardboard envelope. For want of anything better to do, Jill took it out and pushed it into the drive-slot. The machine whirred gently and a pattern of symbols and words unfurled slowly on the screen.

Jill wasn't a computer enthusiast, but she had done some word-processing at school and understood that Tad had been using his computer for this. She knew that the columns of words on the screen were the titles of texts stored in the computer's memory.

ANIMALS	CARVING	CHRISTMAS
BIRDS	CEILING	CLOTHES
CAVE	CHAPEL	CONSPIRACY
CHASM	GLEN	COTTAGE
HILL	STAIR	FLIGHT
INSECTS	TOWER	QUEEN
POOLS	TREES	ROMANES
REPTILES	WEAPONS	

Jill was really no keener to read from a computer screen than she was from a book. If, at that moment, a ray of sunshine had fallen into the room, she would have flicked the switch and run downstairs to the garden. Instead the wind rattled the window and raindrops ran down the glass like tears. So she moved the cursor idly to ROMANES, and when the computer invited her to press "Enter," she did. Too late she realised, with a gasp of alarm, that once again something very odd was happening.

Jill had time to wonder whether the computer had turned into a television, so that again she was seeing herself on screen. But then the frame seemed to dissolve, the picture grew rapidly to life size and she found herself standing on the spiral stair, actually dressed in the clothes she'd been wearing in the film. Peculiarly, after the first shock she didn't feel afraid. It was curiosity that gripped her as she stared in through an open door.

The room, one floor below the flat, was furnished, and seemed smaller than when empty. It was also darker, because it was lined with wainscot, dark polished wood. The poor light from a small, half-shuttered window was only slightly boosted by the fire and a smoky candle on an oak table. In the flickering shadows, Jill made out a large cupboard against one wall. Its doors were open, and its shelves full of bottles and jars. There were rushes scattered on the stone floor and Jill noticed a sour, stuffy smell.

Most interestingly, the room was occupied. At the table, her face half turned away from Jill, a young woman sat in an ornately carved chair. She was wearing a dress similar in style to Jill's, but of much finer material— russet brocade with a pointed bodice embroidered with golden flowers. There were tiny acorn buttons on the sleeves and a creamy ruff at the neck.

For a moment Jill couldn't fathom why this person was familiar, but then it came to her that it was the dress she recognised. She had seen it in a portrait in Tad's film, worn by a young mother holding her baby. She must be Lady Romanes.

Lady Romanes was busy, writing swiftly with a quill pen. Jill, watching her winding up tendrils of dark hair with her left hand and pushing them under her stiff cap, felt like someone in the audience at a play. The curtain had gone up and the interesting question was, what would happen next? What did happen made her gape with astonishment.

Across the room a door opened in the wainscot and Tad came in. He was wearing the same brown and fawn clothes he had worn in the film, and Jill could hear his heavy shoes creaking as he walked across the floor. He was carrying a tray with a silver jug and a glass goblet. Quietly he stepped up to the table and laid the tray at Lady Romanes' elbow. She glanced up, murmured something that Jill couldn't hear and went on writing. Tad poured some wine into the goblet, bowed and moved away.

What a surprise he'll get if he sees me here, thought Jill, willing him to look. But when Tad did look, she had the extraordinary impression that he wasn't surprised at all. With one hand on the iron door latch he paused, turned and looked straight across at Jill. She saw him grin, wink and wiggle his fingers in a comical greeting. Before she could respond he went out and shut the door.

Suddenly Jill had a feeling in her chest that was both happiness and pain. More than anything she wanted to run across the room, open the door and call, "Tad! Wait for me!"

But it was impossible. As she struggled to move forward, it was as if a glass wall prevented her. The room shrank and the frame of the computer screen reappeared. Jill had a final glimpse of Lady Romanes before finding herself once again sitting at Tad's desk. Blowing out her cheeks in sheer amazement, she switched off the machine.

7

Looking for Lady Romanes

For once, Jill was glad that her father had so little to say at meal times, because at lunch she wasn't in the mood for conversation either. While he ate his boiled egg and read the newspaper, she ate hers and stared through the window at the coiling mist. When he made a mug of coffee and took it away to the office, she scarcely noticed that he was gone.

Jill had never really believed in the supernatural, but it was clear to her that she would now have to change her mind. Obviously in this ancient place the past was getting mixed up with the present—apparently through the video camera and the computer—although how these electronic devices could call up such extraordinary images was really beyond comprehension. To have seen someone alive in the sixteenth century was breathtaking enough, yet even more astounding surely was that Jill and Tad had been there too. It surprised Jill, who in the beginning had been so terrified, that now she was far more intrigued than afraid.

When she had finished eating, a deep curiosity made Jill pull on a jersey and go downstairs to the room where, that morning and four centuries ago, Tad had served wine to Lady Romanes. Nothing of the room she had seen earlier remained, except for the stone fireplace. The wainscot was gone and so was the furniture. The window was a hole in the wall, and the door through which Tad had appeared was the entrance to another, equally dreary room. Jill ran her fingers over the stone and looked up the draughty chimney, but she knew she was wasting her time. If this had ever been Lady Romanes' room, there was no trace of her now.

The air was chilly, and suddenly Jill felt oppressed by the past she could not longer see. She shivered and thought how nice it would be to warm herself upstairs by the electric fire. She was on her way out when her eye was caught by an inscription round the top of the door.

Mr Weaver had mentioned that a lot of restoration work had been done in the castle during the last year, and the carved letters over the doorway had obviously received recent attention. They were painted gold against a background of white and green.

RR:KA ♥ SEMPER FIDELIS:1561

Jill had no idea what this meant, but she was determined to find out. There were other questions in her mind too, and on reflection she decided that this time it would be safe to put them to her father.

Jill expected to have to wait until evening, when Mr Weaver would have finished work. When she got to the top of the stair, however, she noticed that the office door was ajar. On impulse she pushed it open and looked into the cramped room where her father sat at a desk as untidy as Tad's was immaculate.

"Do you mind being interrupted?" she asked, and was relieved when he put down his ballpoint, grinned widely and said, "I love it. What can I do for you?"

Jill went and leant on her elbow against the desk.

"Dad," she began. "Remember that Lady Romanes in the portrait in the film, the one with a baby in a little white cap? Can you tell me anything about her?"

She saw a delighted expression appear on her father's tanned face.

"What is it about this place?" he laughed. "First Tad, now you. And they say young people aren't interested in the past!"

Jill, unable to explain that it was the past that seemed interested in her, let this pass.

"OK, but do you know about her?" she persisted.

Mr Weaver pursed his lips, then shook his head.

"Not a lot," he admitted. "Tad's the expert on the Romanes. All I know is that her name was Kate, and she was a herbalist."

"What's that?"

"Someone who grows plants and makes medicines from them," her father explained. "Odd you should mention her, actually. I'm restoring the garden from a plan she made. I found it in an old book in the National Library. I'll let you see it, if you like."

"Mmm. Thanks," murmured Jill, but she was thinking of the jars and bottles she had seen in Lady Romanes' cupboard. She must have put her medicines in them, she thought, stunned by the strangeness of it all. "And those letters over the door downstairs," she went on. "Do you know what they mean?"

"Oh, that. RR, Robert Romanes and KA, Katherine Adair," Mr Weaver explained. "Your Lady Romanes again, of course. 'Semper fidelis' is the family motto. Latin for 'always faithful.' "

"I see," said Jill. "Why is there a little heart?"

She saw her father's brown eyes narrow suddenly and his smile vanish.

"Ach, why is there ever a little heart?" he answered impatiently. "They were married in 1561."

Jill knew why he was rattled, and that it would have been kinder to change the subject. But she had always seen the break-up of her parents' marriage as a dirty trick they had played on her, and she couldn't resist saying snidely, "So they really loved each other."

Mr Weaver made a sceptical face.

"If they did, it was a bonus," he retorted. "People like them didn't marry for love, Jill; they married for money.

Kate Adair was a wealthy lass, and she brought Lord Romanes a fine dowry."

Jill couldn't think of a reply to this, and when her father abruptly pulled some papers towards him she turned away. As she was closing the door, however, he called her back. She saw him looking amiable and remembered that his annoyance never lasted long.

"Listen," he said. "I reckon Tad could tell you a lot more about the Romanes than I can. If you're interested, why don't you give him a ring in the evening and ask him?"

"I'm not *that* interested," replied Jill coldly.

The following afternoon, when the sun had returned and she was helping Mrs Bowden in the little shop, Jill found a reproduction of Lady Romanes' portrait among the postcards for sale. Under the picture were the words: "Lady Katherine Romanes with her son Archibald, by Hans Eworth, circa, 1562."

"Do you know what *circa* means?" she asked Mrs Bowden.

She preferred not to ask her father, who had been rather distant since she snubbed him about Tad.

"I suppose it means 'round about,' " said Mrs Bowden, glancing at the card. "Bonny lass, isn't she?"

Jill thought so too. She bought the postcard and pinned it up beside her bed. And as if to remind her, during the next few days the initials of Robert Romanes and his young wife kept recurring, on the wall of the roofless chapel, among the angels on the painted ceiling, entwined with verdigris leaves on a copper sundial in the garden.

Meanwhile the computer stood idle on Tad's desk, and although Jill sometimes looked at it speculatively she wasn't inclined to touch it. At least, not until the evening of the next wet day.

8

Full Face

It had been the most shatteringly tedious day Jill had spent since she arrived at Gryffe. She had woken to a dour tattoo of rain on the roof; her father had departed immediately after breakfast to attend a meeting in Edinburgh, and at eleven o'clock Mrs Bowden had rung up to say there was no point in opening the shop. No one, she rightly predicted, would want to visit a castle in such weather. Jill spent the day petulantly flicking from one television channel to another and feeling like a rat in a cage. By evening she was ready to scream with boredom.

This was the only reason why, after her bath, she found herself looking at the computer and wondering whether she might risk pressing "Enter" again. As a diversion, another glimpse into the past seemed rather enticing.

All the same, Jill hesitated. As she brushed her hair and put on her nightie, she seemed to hear two voices in her head offering different advice. One pointed out that what had happened last time was extremely spooky and might even be dangerous; you ought not to be able to see your brother, who was spending the summer in Ealing, serving wine to a woman who had been dead for four centuries. On the other hand, a second voice reminded her, although the experience had been strange, it hadn't been at all terrifying. Jill had only been a spectator, first of the video film, then of the scene in Lady Romanes' room. True, she had been briefly aware of her body itching inside a tight, scratchy gown, and her toes being pinched by hard leather. But—reassuringly—when she had wanted to go in she hadn't been able to, and had immediately been returned to the present. It would be thrilling to have another glimpse of Lady Romanes, whose beautiful oval face on the postcard was becoming as familiar to Jill as her mother's. Jill wouldn't admit that it was Tad she most of all wanted to see.

In the end, of course, she listened to the second voice. Quickly she switched on the computer and fed Tad's disc into the drive-slot. When the menu of titles appeared, she again positioned the cursor beside ROMANES, pressed "Enter" and waited tensely for the frame to dissolve.

Only it didn't. There was a long pause while the computer seemed to consider its options, then it beeped and the screen went blank. Jill was so disappointed that she didn't even bother to switch it off, but flounced furiously into bed. Surprisingly, she fell instantly asleep.

When Jill woke she had no idea of the time, but it was dark, and to her drowsy annoyance something prickly was sticking into her hip. Crossly she squirmed over, only to feel a worse prickle at her shoulder. Turning again, she stretched her legs—and realised that the bed had changed. Instead of lying on a smooth mattress, she was rolling about on something that shifted and rustled and pricked her tender skin. Its smell told her that it was a sack of straw, and when she groped for the duvet she found that it had become a hairy blanket.

Jolted into wakefulness, Jill sat bolt upright. She wanted to jump out of bed and run to find her father, but before she could events had moved on. Outside her window lights erupted, sending a wash of reflected pink and orange across the ceiling. In the glow Jill saw that her room had changed. Tad's desk, computer and bookshelves had disappeared. Instead, between Jill's bed and the window were two more wooden cribs, each with a sleeping occupant. Jill shivered, not only because suddenly it was bitterly cold.

She was scared, but also curious. Hearing the sharp clip-clop of horses' hoofs and men's voices in the courtyard, she slipped out of bed. Weaving around the sleepers on silent feet she once again jumped up on the window sill. When she looked down, she was amazed.

The door at the foot of the stair was open, and light spilled across cobbles unexpectedly laced with glittering frost. There were boys with torches, tawny flames leaping fiercely on the ends of wooden poles. Three men were dismounting from horses. As they slouched towards the door others darted from the shadows to grab the horses' bridles and lead them away. Jill watched the torchbearers vanish round a corner and the door was closed.

Later she would think how silly she had been, but at the time Jill longed to share what was happening with her father. If he was involved, her terrible burden of loneliness would at last be eased. Eagerly she jumped down from the sill, stealthily opened the door and groped for the latch on his.

"Dad," she whispered, peeping round the edge.

There was no reply. Mr Weaver's pine bedstead was gone, and so, apparently, was Mr Weaver. This room too seemed to have become a dormitory with humped figures sleeping on sacks on the floor. Someone was snuffling softly, and when one of the sleepers grunted and turned over, Jill shut the door in a panic. Anxiously she groped her way along the passage. A primitive and stinking lavatory opened where she expected the sitting-room, and the kitchen was a storeroom, full of fruit baskets and sacks of meal. There was an open arch to the stair, very faintly lit from below. Creeping down, Jill again reached the entrance to Lady Romanes' room.

Katherine Romanes was in her nightgown, a dark blue velvet robe. She had drawn her chair close to the fire, and in candlelight Jill again saw her face in profile, bordered now by long dark hair. Jill, who was button-nosed and rosy-cheeked, looked admiringly at the straight, pale features. Then Lady Romanes turned and gave her the worst shock of her life.

Jill could scarcely believe it. It looked as if someone had thrown purple paint which had spattered against Lady Romanes' left cheekbone, staining her eye socket and running in dark streaks down to her chin. The discoloured skin was thick and scaly, and fiery where it strained against the white skin around it. It looked so sore that tears of sympathy welled in Jill's eyes; awareness that Lady Romanes could see her added to her embarrassment. Surprisingly, however, Lady Romanes didn't behave as if she had been caught out by a stranger. She smiled as if Jill were someone she knew.

"Not *still* awake?" she said, and as Jill hesitated held out her hand. "Come, then," she added, "before you freeze to death in your shift."

The moment she heard the soft, gutteral Scots voice, Jill stopped being afraid. This time no invisible wall stopped her, and she pattered over the rush-strewn floor to Lady Romanes' side. The warmth of the fire was pleasant, and it seemed natural to lean on the arm of the chair with her face close to the purple cheek. There was a lemony scent on the thick brown hair.

"Does your face hurt?" Jill asked gently, wondering too late if it was rude to mention it.

She was relieved that Lady Romanes didn't seem to think so.

"The frost makes it ache," she admitted, but then changed the subject. "Why are you not asleep?" she asked.

"I was," answered Jill truthfully, "but a noise woke me. Horses' feet and men talking in the yard."

Lady Romanes sighed.

"I heard them too," she said. "It is Master Rollo, my lord's brother, home from France for the Christmas holidays. Never one to do anything quietly."

The tartness in her voice made it clear that Lady Romanes didn't much care for Master Rollo.

"How long will he stay?" ventured Jill.

Lady Romanes shrugged her narrow shoulders.

"Till after the Queen leaves, I suppose," she said. "However long, it will seem longer."

Jill wasn't sure how to respond, so she said, "I just hope he didn't wake your baby."

Lady Romanes smiled.

"He will have his cousin, Flora, to reckon with if he woke Archy," she replied.

Jill was now completely out of her depth. She was silent for a moment, then surprised herself.

"Kate," she heard her own voice saying plaintively, "why can't I sleep in your room, like I did when we lived at Drumspynie?"

Immediately she could have kicked herself. What an idiot I am, she thought. Certainly she had never heard of a place called Drumspynie in her life. So the kindly but firm answer surprised her too.

"Because when we lived at Drumspynie I was unwed, and you were a little child. Now I am a wife, and what would my husband say if my maid were lying in a crib at our feet? We must just be glad that we are still together, you and I."

"I am glad, Kate," Jill said.

Warm after being so cold, she felt very sleepy. Her head lolled against the scented hair. Lady Romanes steadied her.

"Bed," she said, getting to her feet, "or else you will be too tired tomorrow to go and help fetch home the Yule log. I have told your brother you will be ready at noon."

"My brother?" mumbled Jill, now almost asleep on her feet. "Do you mean Tad?"

Lady Romanes chuckled and rumpled Jill's hair with a long, ringed hand.

"I mean Master Thaddeus Webster, known to you and me as Tad," she said. "How many brothers do you have, Mistress Sleepyhead? Now come. I shall take you up, or you will surely fall asleep on the stair."

Meekly Jill took her hand, and allowed herself to be pulled upstairs and along the dark passage.

"Quietly, or we shall wake Lilly and Bess," warned Lady Romanes in a whisper as she opened the door.

She waited until Jill had climbed onto the rustling sack and twitched the blanket over her. Then she drew an invisible cross on Jill's forehead with her thumb and went away.

9

Historical Twins

Back in July next morning, Jill put her head round the office door and said, "Dad, have you ever heard of a place called Drumspynie?"

She knew she was taking a risk. Mr Weaver might still be feeling sore with her. If he raised his eyebrows and said, "What on earth makes you ask that?" she wouldn't know how to reply. Fortunately he looked up from his calculator, smiled and said, "Still researching, are you?"

"Yes," answered Jill.

"Drumspynie's up north in Aberdeenshire," her father told her. "That Lady Kate Adair you were asking about was the daughter of an Earl of Spynie, and the Drumspynie estates passed to the Romanes family through her descendants. Which was a pity for Gryffe, because the minute the Romanes got their mitts on Drumspynie off they went, leaving this poor old place to fall to pieces."

"I see," said Jill, trying to sound more nonchalant than she felt. "Have you ever been there?"

Mr Weaver nodded.

"Yes. Tad and I had a jaunt in the Easter holidays to visit it. It's beautiful, one of those tall, golden castles with turrets and a stunning garden."

"Does anyone live there?"

"Not now. The last Romanes sold it about 1840 to people called Cameron, and they gave it to the National Trust for Scotland in the 1960s."

Sounds like Amanda's place, thought Jill, and couldn't help feeling amused. It had gone through her mind more than once that Amanda's holiday adventures hadn't been a patch on her own. But meantime Mr Weaver had risen from his desk.

"Hang on a minute," he said. "I think I still have the Drumspynie guide book."

"Great," said Jill.

She waited expectantly while he selected a box file from his metal shelves and riffled through the contents. But disappointment followed.

"Not here, I'm afraid," said Mr Weaver apologetically. "Tad must've taken it away with him."

Damn, thought Jill. She wanted to say, "What on earth for?" but stopped herself in time. "Well, thanks anyway," she said.

She would have gone then, but Mr Weaver said suddenly, "Talking of Kate Adair—I meant to tell you. The other day I remembered Tad saying he'd found out she was disabled in some way. Maybe he said she was a hunchback, or only had one eye. I was busy with something, and I don't exactly recall."

But I do, thought Jill as she closed the door, the image of Lady Romanes' terribly damaged face clear in her mind's eye.

It was another fine day, so Jill went out and climbed Gryffe hill to her favourite spot beside the pool. She took off her shoes and socks, and as she dabbled her feet in the green water she thought over what had happened last night, and her conversation with her father. It was astonishing to find that a place she had mentioned without ever having heard of it did exist, though no stranger than other things that had happened. More interesting to Jill at the moment was her own role in the mystery.

Quite clearly, she thought, Lady Romanes had known her last night, and known her well. She hadn't even tried to conceal her hurt face as one would from a stranger. Equally clearly, the Jill she had recognised as a friend couldn't possibly be the girl who was now, on a summer morning, paddling in a pool on Gryffe hill. It was a case of mistaken identity. But how so? Jill took her feet out of the water and lay down on the warm grass to let the sun dry them. For a few moments she felt completely bamboozled, then slowly an explanation began to form in her mind.

Long ago, in the sixteenth century, there must have lived another Jill, to whom modern Jill was identical. A sort of historical twin. What was it Lady Romanes had called Tad? "Master Thaddeus Webster." So his sister's name must have been Jill Webster. And since twentieth-century Tad and Jill were both called Weaver, surely this meant that Tad too was inside the body of a historical twin. How he had got back to Gryffe, all the way from Lessington Avenue, Ealing, Jill couldn't imagine—yet when she considered, she realised that this didn't matter. If you were going to do anything as stupendous as travelling through time, it hardly mattered where you started from.

Jill put on her shoes and socks again and walked slowly home. The church clock was striking noon, its sound clear on the breeze, as she went upstairs to her room. As she opened the door a faint humming drew her attention to the computer, and she was aware that it had been switched on since last night without her noticing. She went to turn it off, but as she extended her hand over the keyboard, her forefinger touched the "Enter" key.

Jill would have sworn it was accidental, but before she had time for more than an impatient tut she was again standing on the stair outside Lady Romanes' room. A blast of icy air blew upwards, and when she looked down she saw a long grey cloak and skirt where her cotton shorts had been. A moment later, as she clattered into the courtyard, a flurry of snowflakes danced out of a steely sky.

10

The Yule Log

"So you've arrived," said Tad, side-stepping piles of reeking horse droppings as he crossed the cobbles towards Jill. "I was just coming to fetch you."

He spoke casually, as if they had parted only yesterday. Too bewildered by the swiftness of her arrival to reply, Jill let him draw her into a corner sheltered from the biting wind. She was used to seeing the courtyard empty, swept as clean as the kitchen floor and with baskets of geraniums hanging on its broken walls. Now it was full of people in sixteenth-century dress, noisy children playing tag, men lounging against high, crenellated walls that shut out most of the sky. Dogs scrapped and yelped, while a pinched, ragged boy tried to calm a nervously whinnying pony between the shafts of a wooden cart.

At length Jill managed to ask, "What's happening, Tad?"

"We're waiting for Master Rollo," replied Tad sourly, rubbing his cherry-red nose. "This is supposed to be a holiday when we have fun bringing home the Yule log and holly to decorate the great hall, but now that my lord has put that sadistic lout in charge—" He shrugged and blew on his purple fingers to warm them. "Are you sure you want to come?" he asked anxiously.

Jill nodded vigorously. What Tad said was alarming, but she was sure she wanted to stick with him. She also wanted to ask him questions, but just as she opened her mouth the atmosphere in the courtyard changed. Games stopped abruptly, loungers straightened up and silence fell.

"Here we go," muttered Tad as a tall, youngish man emerged from the doorway at the foot of the stair. Apart from a thin white ruff he was all in black, and as Jill watched him surveying the yard with small, glittering blue eyes Tad's feelings began to infect her.

"Tad," she whispered, but before she could go on Rollo Romanes let out a roar.

"Move on, then, before I freeze to death. You, George Seton! Help the brat with the cart. Torkel MacInnes, stay in the rear and kick any dolt who lags behind. We go to the wood at Simpleside."

"Merry Christmas," whispered Tad sarcastically as Rollo pulled his fur-lined cloak around him and strode towards the gate.

A subdued, untidy procession formed behind the cart. As she left the yard with Tad, Jill looked wonderingly at a scene which was recognisable, yet quite different in detail from the one she knew. There was a drawbridge over a filthy green moat. The chapel was thatched with what looked like turf. The wood, instead of being a straggle of thin oak beside the Clathy burn, stretched greyly westward until it vanished round the side of the hill. The burn itself hadn't changed, although there were stepping stones instead of a bridge, and Jill heard the familiar roar of the torrent as it toppled into the gorge.

Before long, however, her attention focussed on her own plight. Wedged into an ill-humoured, jostling crowd, Jill had to slither down a mudslide of a road while the east wind puffed snow maliciously into her face. She hadn't gone a hundred metres before her hands and feet were numb, and she thought she was the one who would freeze to death. Only when she noticed the ragged tunics and holed stockings of two shivering waifs in front, she felt ashamed.

"Pity he ever came back," growled a voice behind.

"Pity he was ever born," retorted another, and there was an angry murmur of agreement.

Down the glen at Simpleside, where in another time the Bowdens would have their farm, a thicket of holly and oak leaned into the wintry hillside. By the time they reached it Jill, like the other children, was too wretched to do anything but huddle under the bare branches. The men and the older boys, including Tad, set to work with axes and knives.

First a large tree trunk went into the cart, then branches of holly, strands of ivy and bunches of mistletoe. Glumly Jill watched Rollo Romanes strutting in his warm cloak, barking orders, finding fault. Some Christmas holiday, she thought.

Going back was even worse. The cart was too heavy for the poor pony, and progress uphill was very slow. Perversely Rollo wouldn't let anyone go ahead of the cart, and when the clouds turned sallow and snow set in seriously, a pall of misery lay over the company.

Jill plodded along beside Tad, who was trying to shelter a thin girl called Lilly under his grey tweed cloak. He had hardly spoken since they set out, and Jill knew from the frown between his eyebrows that something serious was worrying him. Her own feet were soaking and her hood was full of melting snow, but at least the lights of the castle were now appearing through the gloom. She was taken by surprise when Rollo suddenly loomed up beside Tad and tweaked his cap back from his face.

"Ah, Master Webster! My lady's fool!" he cried, baring yellow teeth in a broad smile.

Then without warning he shot out his fist and gave Tad a vicious clout on the ear.

Tad slipped, and both he and Lilly fell in the slushy mud. Jill was momentarily disbelieving, then absolutely furious. She had clenched her own fists and was poised to launch herself on Rollo Romanes when Tad scrambled to his feet and threw himself in front of her.

"Don't be stupid, Jill," he hissed, at which his attacker burst out laughing.

"It would be stupid indeed," he agreed, and walked away quickly towards the castle.

Tears were running down Jill's cheeks, but Tad said, "It doesn't matter, honestly. He's vile to everyone, and he hates me because he knows I'm for Kate."

"For Kate?" repeated Jill, bewildered. "Who against?"

They were back in the courtyard. Lilly had disappeared, and in the early dusk men were unloading the cart outside the tower door. Those not needed had dispersed thankfully, leaving Jill and Tad alone.

"Listen. We have to talk," said Tad urgently. "I think Kate's in danger—from that man. I know—why don't we go up to Kate's room now? She'll have gone to the nursery to visit Archy, and my lord never calls me till after five. No one will disturb us there."

He walked purposefully towards the door, and with her heart beating very fast Jill followed.

11

An Alarming Tale

Just in case the room wasn't empty, Tad tapped on the door and cautiously put his nose round the edge.

"All clear," he reported to Jill and they slipped in, closing the door quietly behind them.

Jill was thankful to see a peat fire glowing on the hearth. She crouched beside it while Tad lit a candle and jammed it onto a spiked candlestick on the table.

"Take off your shoes and stockings," he said. "We may as well get them dried while we have a chance."

Jill's feet felt horrible, and she gladly agreed. When their wet footwear was laid out on the warm hearthstone she and Tad sat among the dusty rushes, holding out their hands to the heat. Jill glanced sideways at Tad. His pointed, freckled face was intense under his thatch of bright hair, and for all her alarm Jill enjoyed a moment

63

of fervent happiness because here they were together, and friends. She had been longing to discuss with Tad the theory she had worked out about historical twins, but now she had forgotten. "Tell me what's happened, Tad," she begged instead.

Tad shifted his position and extended his bare feet towards the fire. He was silent for a moment, then said slowly, "I'm not sure what you know already. Being with Kate such a lot, you probably don't hear as much talk as I do."

"I hardly know anything," said Jill truthfully.

Tad nodded.

"Well, then," he said. "It's well known that Master Rollo grew up assuming that he would be Lord Romanes' heir. Although they're brothers, Rollo's twenty years younger, and no one thought my lord would ever marry. So when he married Kate at the age of fifty, it must've been a hellish blow for Rollo. Of course he had to pretend to be pleased, and I dare say he just hoped there would be no children. But when Archy was born in September it must have seemed that his chance of being Lord Romanes was gone for good."

"So?" prompted Jill, the fireglow reflected in her round, wondering eyes.

Tad flipped over their steaming stockings as if he were cooking bacon.

"He took it badly," he replied. "He was always too uppity to be likeable, but after Archy's appearance he got really nasty. Apparently he even tried to get compensation from his brother for what he said was a dirty trick that had been played on him. When my lord refused, Rollo lost his temper and made some unwise remarks about Kate's appearance. There was an awful row and Lord Romanes gave him the thrashing of his life."

Jill found this satisfying for more than one reason.

"So Lord Romanes really does love Kate," she said, remembering the little heart.

"Yes," agreed Tad. "Like you and me, he sees more of her than her face." He paused, then went on, "Anyway— after that Master Rollo was sent off to France to cool down, giving us all a bit of peace. But as today's performance made clear, he didn't stay away long enough."

Jill was fascinated, but also confused.

"You said Kate was in danger from Rollo," she said. "If Lord Romanes loves her, how can that be?"

Tad's brows met in a ferocious frown.

"Last night when Rollo arrived," he told Jill, "he had supper in private with Lord Romanes. I waited on them and heard their conversation. You wouldn't believe how sweet and reasonable Rollo was, saying how good it was to be home, asking how his nephew Archy was, and how much he'd grown. I felt sick, but Lord Romanes was charmed by him. Only later, when my lord had gone to bed, I overheard Master Rollo singing a very different song."

"How come?"

Tad again turned the stockings, which were beginning to singe.

"I'd finished my chores and gone up to bed," he told Jill. "I was in the privy at the end of our passage having a pee when I heard footsteps on the stair. I only had my shirt on, so I peeped through a knothole in the door to see who it was before I came out. There were two people. One of them wasn't in my line of vision, but the other was Master Rollo. He has a nasty habit of cuffing my ear, so I kept very quiet and hoped they'd go away."

"Did they?"

"No. They stepped into the storeroom doorway and I could hear what they were saying. They were talking about Kate."

"About Kate?" Jill's eyes widened further. "What did they say?"

Tad gulped as if he were recalling a nightmare.

"Rollo said they must start a rumour that Kate had killed the miller's boy and got rid of his body by magic," he replied. "He said that if people blamed her for that, then when the deed was done they'd blame her for it too. The other man said the rumour had started already, my lady looking so witchlike, which made Rollo guffaw like mad. He said the other man had done well so far, and if he kept his mouth shut and did as he was told, he would be well rewarded."

Jill hadn't a clue what Tad was talking about.

"I don't understand," she said. "What does it all mean?"

Tad clicked his tongue impatiently.

"Isn't it obvious?" he said. "Rollo is up to mischief.

He's planning to do something rotten and shift the blame onto Kate—presumably to punish her for marrying his brother and producing a baby boy. Meanwhile, he's going to spread a rumour that she's a witch, which is not only wicked. It's very dangerous."

At the word *witch*, Jill's chest went tight, and she saw the firelit room through a blur of fear. Although she usually thought of witches as figures of Halloween fun, she knew that when people had really believed in their power, the accused had been treated with shocking cruelty. She licked her lips and at last managed to say, "What happened to the miller's boy?"

Tad raised his eyebrows, as if he were surprised that Jill should ask. But then he went on quickly, "The answer is, nobody knows. A few days ago his mother sent him up the glen to the castle to ask Kate for some ginger syrup for his father's cough. He never arrived. Lord Romanes thinks he must have slipped in the glen and fallen into a pool or down a crevice. We all went searching, but his body hasn't been found."

Jill had a sudden, poignant memory of the gentle young woman who had called her "Mistress Sleepyhead" and blessed her before she fell asleep.

"But surely," she cried passionately, "no one would seriously believe that Kate—"

"Oh yes, they would," Tad interrupted harshly. "The people here are superstitious and ignorant, and that makes them cruel. For all the kindness Kate shows them, they would believe it, all right."

Jill shuddered.

"What can we do?" she asked.

Tad drew his knees up to his chin and hugged them with his thin arms.

"I'm not sure yet," he admitted. "I can't tell Lord Romanes what I heard because he'd never take my word against his brother's, and I can't tell Kate because I don't want to scare her to death. But—" his voice grew resolute "—we must find some way of protecting her. After all she's done for us, taking us in when we were left orphans, and educating us and getting us places here in Lord Romanes' household, we can't let that dirty rat destroy her."

Jill thought this was a brave speech. So it seemed a bit unfair when, just at that moment, the latch clicked and a displeased voice spoke behind them.

"And what are you two imps doing here, I'd liked to know?" it said.

12

Mistress Wysse

Jill jumped. Looking nervously over her shoulder, she saw Lady Romanes standing in the doorway. She was wearing a dark green dress with a yellow taffeta under-skirt, and her hair was drawn back under a stiff lace cap. Jill thought that without loose hair shading it the lop-sided, discoloured face looked more painful than ever. She was startled by Tad's speedy scrambling to his feet, but reckoned she'd better get up too. When Tad bowed she surprised herself by curtseying, for the first time in her life.

Lady Romanes walked over to the table and put down a leather bag. She looked without a trace of a smile at her uninvited visitors and said, "Well?"

Jill shifted awkwardly from one bare foot to the other, and left it to Tad to explain as well as he could.

"I beg your pardon, my lady," he said contritely. "We were cold and wet, and knowing that you would be with Master Archibald we took the liberty—"

"Exactly," interrupted Lady Romanes emphatically. "Using my room without permission is a liberty, and one I prefer you not to repeat. Do you understand, Tad?"

"Yes, my lady."

"And why?"

"I think so, my lady."

"Then we shall say no more. But for God's sake, child, try to remember. We are not at Drumspynie now."

Lady Romanes glanced at the shoes and stockings lying on the hearth and gestured to Jill and Tad to put them on. While they did so, grimacing at the clammy touch of damp wool, she went over to her cupboard and took down a large jar.

"Be off with you, Tad," she said abruptly, and Jill had to watch helplessly as Tad rammed his flat bonnet onto his head and picked up his cloak.

"Don't say a word," he whispered, and disappeared through the door in the wainscot.

Between fatigue and anxiety Jill was close to tears.

Lady Romanes took a wooden spatula and transferred a dollop of minty green ointment from the large jar to a small one. Jill watched as she put a scrap of cloth over the small jar and tied it on with a wisp of red thread.

"This salve is for Mistress Wysse's chilblains," she said. "I want you to take it to her. I have told her how often to use it, so you will not have a message to forget."

Jill didn't know whether this was a joke or not, and she was afraid to admit that she neither knew who Mistress Wysse was nor where to find her. Her tears overflowed.

"My lady, please don't be angry," she sobbed.

Lady Romanes raised her head, and even in her own distress Jill was shocked by the misery in the strange brown eyes. Could Lady Romanes know already what evil people were saying about her? Certainly she was upset about something.

"Nay, Jill, I am not angry," she said, also on the verge of tears. "Would I raise lambs with my own hand, then drive them away from my hearth? I know it seems hard, but Tad is now a servant of Lord Romanes, and though I love you, I must not be seen to spoil you. Try to understand."

Jill sniffed and wiped her eyes on her coarse woollen sleeve.

"Yes, my lady," she said.

"Here, then." Lady Romanes forced a smile as she put the tiny aromatic pot into Jill's hand. "Run with this to Mistress Wysse and hurry back. We shall have time for music before supper."

She pushed Jill gently towards the door that Tad had used, and because she had to, Jill went. She found herself in a firelit bedroom; a fierce glow illuminated a four-poster bed with red curtains, and tapestried walls. There was another door across the rush-strewn floor, and because she couldn't go back Jill opened it a fraction and peeped out. To her vast relief she saw Tad sitting on the step.

"Thank goodness you waited," breathed Jill, slumping down weakly beside him.

"I can't stay long." Tad glanced up and down the stone-flagged passage, then continued in a low voice, "Listen. Tonight I'm on duty, but tomorrow Torkel waits on my lord, and I am to help decorate the great hall for Christmas. Ask Kate if you can come too, and we'll find an opportunity to slip away and talk. All right?"

"Well, probably," said Jill, wondering privately whether by that time she might not be sitting on Gryffe hill in the summer sunshine.

She heard the uncertainty in her own voice, but Tad didn't seem to notice.

"Good," he said, getting to his feet and looking down at the little pot Jill was carrying. "What's that?" he asked.

"It's salve for Mistress Wysse's chilblains," explained Jill. "Tad—"

But Tad interrupted, scowling furiously.

"That old monster?" he hissed. "I wish she had a chilblain on her nose."

"Is she so bad?" asked Jill, startled by his vehemence.

"So bad?" Tad's green eyes narrowed like an angry cat's. "She only got to be Archy's nurse because she's Lord Romanes' cousin, and kept house for him before he married. She's so jealous of Kate, I think she'd stop her seeing her own baby if she could. And now Kate's giving her ointment for her chilblains! It would make you sick."

Jill took this information in, but her own problem was uppermost in her mind.

"Tad," she said urgently. "I don't know the way to Mistress Wysse's room."

Just as when she had asked what had happened to the miller's boy, Jill had a fleeting impression that she had flummoxed Tad. There was a perceptible pause before he burst out laughing.

"Honestly," he said teasingly, "you are the limit. We've been at Gryffe for nearly two years and you still can't find your way around!" But when he saw Jill looking upset he added hastily, "Never mind. Go to the end of this passage and turn left. Go up the stair and turn right. The nursery's the room beyond the candle sconce."

Jill sighed with relief.

"Thanks, Tad," she said.

"See you tomorrow, then," he replied.

Again Jill said, "Probably."

She hurried off down the passage, and following Tad's instructions found her way to the nursery door.

There was a pause before her knock was answered by a squat, middle-aged woman in a stiff brown dress. Her ruff propped up a heavy double chin and her pouchy eyes peered over a flat nose and glum, froglike mouth.

"What do you want?" she asked impatiently.

Jill felt it prudent to curtsey again as she held out the jar.

"This is the salve from Lady Romanes, Mistress Wysse," she said politely.

The woman took the jar without a word of thanks and made to shut the door. Before she could manoeuvre her skirt out of the way, however, Jill was able to peep past her into the room. She saw the end of a bed and beside it a carved, hooded cradle. She also saw Rollo Romanes sitting in a chair by the fire.

For a few seconds, before the door slammed, Jill felt absolutely terrified. If she had followed her instinct she would have rushed off in a panic, searching through gloomy corridors and rooms until she found Tad and told him what she had seen. But then common sense reminded her that Mistress Flora Wysse must be Rollo's cousin too, so there needn't be anything sinister about his visiting her. Jill also remembered that Lady Romanes had told her to hurry back; she had already spent time talking to Tad, and after the ticking-off earlier she thought she should avoid further delay.

Still, she was distracted and took a wrong turning at the bottom of the stair. It was like entering a maze, but after much wandering she somehow reached ground level, and emerged unexpectedly into the courtyard through an unfamiliar door. Sleety snow stung her cheeks as she slithered over the cobbles, passing the huge pile of Christmas greenery glistening in the light from the tower door. Shaking water off her skirt she bounded upstairs, and halfway up met her father coming down.

13

Night Thoughts

By the time Jill got to bed that night she was worn out. Since, oddly, she seemed to have returned from the past at exactly the same moment she had gone into it, she then had to endure a second afternoon helping Mrs Bowden in the shop. When her father had suggested a walk over the moor to Gryffe Loch before supper she hadn't liked to refuse, but on the way back had thought her legs would fold under her. At supper she had almost nodded off over her hamburger, and got into bed reckoning that she'd been awake for twenty hours. Now, she thought, she would sleep, and sleep and sleep.

Annoyingly, this wasn't what happened. The instant Jill closed her eyes, a re-run of the afternoon's lurid events began in her head. She felt her stomach tightening and her throat going dry as she recalled the hateful outing to

Simpleside, Rollo Romanes' attack on Tad and her own terror outside the door of Mistress Wysse's room. It had been a horrible experience, and Jill vowed not to repeat it. Never, never, never would she touch Tad's computer again. She knew she had been a fool to tamper with something she'd guessed was dangerous, and that she'd be an even bigger fool if she didn't learn a lesson now. If Kate Romanes had got herself into some kind of trouble four centuries ago, that was just too bad, and as for any pleasure Jill got from being with Tad—was that worth being scared stiff in a spooky old castle with Rollo Romanes slinking around like a nightmare on legs? Do me a favour, thought Jill, hardening her heart.

Yet still the computer fascinated her. Against her will she kept opening her eyes and glancing across at it. Frightened by this lack of self-control, Jill turned over and lay facing the wall. Only then, every time she opened her eyes, she saw the postcard with the mysteriously perfect face of Kate Romanes. The face troubled her so much that she took the card down and pushed it under her pillow. Unfortunately thoughts couldn't be banished so easily.

As she lay in the still summer twilight, pictures formed on the screen behind Jill's closed eyes. She saw herself and Tad, two tiny children in rags, stumbling through a snowstorm towards a tall, turreted castle. She saw herself being lifted by Kate Adair and carried away to be warmed and comforted.

"Dry your eyes, Jill. I always wanted a brother and

sister, so you and Tad will be mine. You will call me Kate, and we shall have such fun together."

For a while, they had had fun. Jill visualised a firelit hall where Tad was playing his lute and she and Kate were dancing. She saw a hedged garden where she and Tad were helping Kate to pick gooseberries and put them in a basket. She seemed to hear shrieks of merriment as she played hide-and-seek with Tad and Kate up and down the winding stairs of Drumspynie. Then one spring day a grave, middle-aged man had come riding into the stable yard . . .

You're imagining all this, Jill told herself furiously, pulling the duvet over her head. Yet it was all so vivid that she couldn't suppress another, more alarming explanation. *This is what Jill Webster might have remembered.*

Jill didn't like this idea at all. She had accepted the idea that she and Jill Webster were identical physically because there seemed no other way of explaining her experiences. The notion of sharing her mind with someone else was much scarier, and Jill burrowed hotly into her bed, desperate to reject it. In the end, though, her effort was in vain.

Try as she might, Jill just couldn't stifle a surge of loyal affection for the brave, disfigured young woman, wrongly accused of a terrible crime and so much in need of friends. Remorse and shame swept over her as she recalled Tad's passionate words: "After all she's done for us . . . we can't let that dirty rat destroy her." Perhaps it was Jill Webster's emotion she was feeling, but suddenly Jill knew that however afraid she was, she must go back—not for Tad's companionship alone, but to help him fight to discredit Rollo and save Kate Romanes.

Jill slipped resolutely out of bed and went to switch on the computer. She heard the familiar whirring as she positioned the cursor and pressed "Enter." Since, as once before, nothing happened immediately, Jill went back to bed. As she drifted into sleep, she heard faraway music and voices and again the sound of hoofs striking the cobbles in the yard.

14

The Holly and the Ivy

"Of course you may go to the hall, my chicken. Christmas Eve is a holiday for you too." Lady Romanes looked up from the letter she was writing to her father and smiled affectionately at Jill. "Bring Tad back with you when the decorating is finished, and we shall have a game of cards after noon."

Jill had been greatly relieved that no question had been asked about her failure to return from her errand to Mistress Wysse the previous day, though puzzled too. Had the real Jill Webster taken her place, she wondered, so that her absence hadn't been noticed? Or did the Gryffe of long ago only come to life again when she entered it? These were interesting questions, but Jill had no time to ponder them. She was just thankful, as her father sometimes said, "for small mercies."

Now she said, "Thank you, my lady," and skipped to the door in her stiff leather shoes. "Will you come and see the hall when it's done?" she added hopefully as she opened it.

"Perhaps," replied Lady Romanes unenthusiastically, dipping her pen into her inkhorn.

Fortunately Jill knew her way to the great hall. Holding up her bulky skirt, she clattered down to the floor below, scuttled through the room that somehow she knew was called the chamber of dais and ran into the hall. The tables where the household dined were folded against the walls as—again Jill knew—was usual during the day, and in the middle of the wide stone floor were heaped the evergreens from Simpleside. The place was cold, for the hearth was swept and empty, awaiting the Yule log. It would be lit that evening, the sign that the Christmas festivities had really begun.

Despite the chill, the hall was full of people enjoying themselves. Pages, maids and grooms were busy with the decorations, laughing and teasing as they filled the alcoves with holly and twined ivy round the candle sconces on the walls. Jill saw Tad up a ladder, hanging sprigs of mistletoe from the minstrels' gallery at the far end of the hall. When he saw Jill he grinned and slithered down.

"We'll slip away now," he said. "There are so many people helping, we won't be missed. Let's go up to the storeroom. We'll be nice and private there."

"Unless Rollo and his friend pay another visit," objected Jill.

Tad shook his head confidently.

"Rollo's ridden to Alloa with my lord," he said. "They won't be back till dusk, so we'll all have an easy day."

It was freezing in the storeroom which in another age would be the Weavers' kitchen, but Tad went and fetched a blanket from the room next to Jill's. The children settled down in a corner among the dusty meal sacks. There was a basket of only slightly rotting apples nearby and they helped themselves.

"Tad, have you any news?" Jill asked eagerly.

She had been looking forward to this moment since she climbed out of her straw bed in the icy morning, pulling on her grey dress over her nightgown and struggling into her thick stockings and shoes. Bess, the older of her roommates, had helped her to put on her cap and Jill had coped with the day so far. She was slightly put out when Tad shook his head doubtfully; she had been confident that by now he'd have worked out what Rollo was up to, and how to foil him.

"Not news, exactly," Tad said. "But I think I know who was in here with Master Rollo two nights ago."

This was something.

"Who?" enquired Jill.

"Torkel MacInnes, my lord's other page."

"What makes you think so?"

Tad spat out a brown bit of apple.

"Torkel sleeps in the same room as me," he said. "Last night when we were going to bed, he couldn't resist showing off a silver coin, a testoon, and hinting that he'd got it from someone who was very pleased with him. I think he wanted us to suppose it was Lord Romanes, but that's very unlikely."

"Why?"

"Because my lord never parts with a penny if he can help it," said Tad bluntly. "He's grousing like mad about what it's going to cost to entertain the Queen. We each had a groat at Michaelmas, and we'll have another tomorrow, and new clothes. But a testoon! That would be the day."

"Hmm," said Jill, not entirely convinced. "That doesn't exactly prove he got it from Rollo," she pointed out.

Tad's smile was close to being a smirk.

"Not by itself," he conceded. "But there's something else. I didn't make the connection at the time, but last night I remembered. Yesterday morning Torkel had flour all over his shoes."

"And?"

"So have we now. There's a burst flour sack over there, beside the door."

Jill looked at the spilt flour, and had to admit that the evidence against Torkel MacInnes was strong.

"So what are we going to do?" she asked.

Tad's smile faded and he shrugged his shoulders. Suddenly he seemed less confident.

"I haven't had time to work out a plan," he admitted. "We'll just have to keep an eye on Rollo and Torkel meantime. At least we know now who the conspirators are."

This seemed a bit feeble to Jill, but she reminded herself that her brother had always been full of bright ideas. Surely he'd have one soon. When he got up she did too, her mind moving abruptly to another matter— her own idea about historical twins. She longed to know what Tad thought about this.

"Listen," she said slowly, "I've been wondering. I know how I got here, but how did you? You're supposed to be spending the summer in Ealing—"

Jill stopped short as Tad stiffened and a frown contracted his gingery brows. For an awful moment she thought he was going to say he didn't know what she was talking about, and stalk huffily away. To her relief he suddenly relaxed and laughed.

"Oh, come on," he said lightly. "Surely we're not going to waste time talking about that—not when so many interesting things are happening here? Wait till I put my blanket back, then we'll go and see how they're getting on in the hall."

So the subject was shelved.

That evening, as she sat at Christmas Eve supper in the great hall, Jill saw Lord Romanes for the first time. A richly dressed, grey-bearded man with bright blue eyes, he sat in a throne-like chair on the dais, a low platform at one end of the hall. On either side was a bench with cushions; Lady Romanes, in her russet and gold dress, sat on his right, and Rollo in sinister black velvet on his left. Mistress Flora Wysse also had a seat at the 'high board.'

Tad, and a thin, sallow youth who must be Torkel, stood behind Lord Romanes with basins, and napkins folded over their arms. From time to time one of them was summoned so that hands could be rinsed and wiped clean.

On either side of Jill and across the hall, other members of Lord Romanes' household, grooms and maids and guardsmen, were having a wonderful party. Tad had mentioned in the afternoon that the twelve days of Christmas were the great fun-festival of the year, when food and drink were plentiful and servants behaved as they'd never dare at any other time.

"Except that this year they will only have six days," Lady Romanes had pointed out with a faint smile, "before they have to begin behaving properly again for the Queen."

If that were so, Jill thought sourly, they were certainly making up for it now. She shuddered as she watched them ripping up goose and venison with dirty fingers, cramming their mouths and gulping wine. They bellowed across the hall to one another, their howls of laughter drowning the music of the sweating pipers and fiddlers in the minstrels' gallery.

In contrast, the people on the dais were silent and unsmiling. Master Rollo and Mistress Wysse glowered and sneered by turns. Lord Romanes had the suffering air that Jill's father assumed at parties, while his wife's strange, discoloured face was expressionless. With a pang of sympathy, Jill thought how hurtful it must be for Lady Romanes to show her face to so many people; from somewhere came a flash of memory reminding her how Lord Spynie had protected his much loved daughter from curious and hostile eyes. If only he were here to protect her now, Jill thought, shivering as she looked at Rollo Romanes. She hoped that Tad was thinking hard.

At long last, the meal was over. The Romanes family departed through a door behind them into the private chamber of dais. In no time the pewter and wooden plates had been stacked, the white cloths whipped off and the tables folded away against the walls. The dogs disposed of the scraps, the minstrels returned to their instruments and the Romanes resumed their seats.

The empty hearth had been filled with twigs, and at a signal from Lord Romanes the musicians struck up merrily. Jill stood watching as the enormous Yule log, twined with ivy, was hauled with ropes down the hall to the fireplace. There was cheering and clapping as Tad, who seemed to be in the thick of everything, came running with a torch which Jill's neighbour at table had said was a fragment of last year's Yule log. The twigs burst into flames and dancing began.

Jill, who had been beckoned by Lady Romanes to sit on the dais at her feet, watched the revels with heavy eyes. Her supper had given her a sore stomach and her head reeled from the hot spiced wine. Glancing up, she was pleased to see that Lord Romanes had his wife's hand in his, but Lady Romanes looked utterly miserable. Again Jill wondered anxiously whether she knew of the terrible rumour circulating in the castle. Jill fervently hoped not, but when, towards midnight, Lord Romanes called for Tad to bring his lute and sing, she was sure that Lady Romanes had tears in her eyes.

Lully lulla, thou little tiny child,
By, by, lully lullay.
O sisters too, how may we do
For to preserve this day
This poor youngling
For whom we do sing,
By, by, lully lullay?

Was she thinking of the miller's lost child, Jill wondered, or of her own little son?

15

Days of Christmas

Although Lady Romanes gave her a silver testoon as a present on Christmas morning, the next three days didn't seem to Jill like Christmas at all. Poor outdoor servants had been drafted in to start cleaning up the castle for the Queen's visit, but for the rest of the men it was the season of amusement. This meant hunting by day and music, dancing and games after supper. After a phantom snowfall there was hard frost, and the dusting of lying snow sparkled like sugar in the sunshine. Tad said it was wonderful hunting weather.

Which was all very well for him, Jill couldn't help thinking rather resentfully. Holed up indoors all day with the kind but distracted Lady Romanes, she brooded a lot on the unfairness of a time when boys seemed to have so much more fun than girls.

Most of the time, Jill had no problem with who she was. She knew that she was Jill Weaver, and believed that when this adventure was over she would return to resume her normal twentieth-century life. But the enclosed atmosphere of Castle Gryffe oppressed her, and sometimes, as she sat by the fire struggling with unfamiliar needlework, her mind seemed to merge disturbingly with that of the girl others supposed her to be.

What she had recognised as "imagining" in bed one night then seemed to be what she really knew about herself: that she and Tad were the orphans of the Earl of Spynie's cowherd, that after the death of their mother they had struggled through a terrible snowstorm to Drumspynie, where Kate Adair had adopted them and brought them up. Jill knew that Lord Spynie had allowed this because he hadn't expected Kate to marry, but of course things had worked out differently. Because Kate was loving and loyal, she had insisted after her marriage on bringing the children to Gryffe—though on Lord Romanes' terms, not her own.

Jill Webster had never liked the grim lowland fortress where she had to call Kate "My lady" and share a cubbyhole with two slovenly kitchen girls, and she hated seeing so little of Tad. But she loved Kate Romanes, and when Jill Weaver grabbed her mind back this feeling of love remained. What was making this Christmas so miserable was knowing that Rollo Romanes was spreading dangerous lies and planning an evil deed.

What was making Christmas also exasperating was that Tad, having worried Jill half to death, was now doing absolutely nothing useful. On Christmas night, when Jill cornered him in the passage outside her room, he was off-hand and evasive. In response to Jill's "Have you had any ideas yet?" he merely shrugged his shoulders.

"I'm thinking about it," he said, then catching Jill's baleful eye added quickly, "Look. Rollo can't do anything till Christmas is past. He and Torkel are out hunting all day, and he's too drunk by evening to do anything but stagger to bed. Next week the Queen will be here, and he wouldn't dare. So why don't we just enjoy ourselves for a bit, eh? Come on—I'll race you to the great hall."

He poked Jill mischievously in the ribs and ran off laughing. Although she was far from satisfied, Jill laughed too and chased after him. As she reached the top of the stair she had a fleeting memory of once watching the scene she was acting out now.

Sadly, Jill didn't have many opportunities to enjoy herself. Every morning after Lady Romanes had said her prayers in the tiny chapel, a dismal queue formed on the stair outside her room. There were kitchen maids with burnt hands, kennel boys with bitten legs, children with boils, rheumaticky old men and women. Lady Romanes treated them all gently, providing bandages and medicine for their troubles, but Jill hated the way they squinted inquisitively, almost gloatingly into her damaged face.

She had seen the same expression in eyes glancing towards the dais during the evening's revelry, and it made her cold with fear.

Lady Romanes was gentle with Jill too, but she was dull company. The only time she ever cheered up was in the afternoon, when she went up to the nursery to visit her baby son. Jill couldn't understand why a three-month-old baby should live separately from his mother, cared for by his father's cousin and fed at the breast of a fat peasant woman. But Tad, who seemed to know everything, had assured her that this was the way of rich folk.

Lady Romanes took Jill with her, and Jill was allowed to hold Archy while his mother unwrapped his clothes and exercised his little arms and legs. He was a jolly baby who giggled a lot, and Jill, who had longed in vain for a little brother or sister, thought he was enchanting. While Lady Romanes chatted to Mistress Wysse she rocked his cradle and made funny noises to see him laugh.

At the same time she watched the two women under her eyelashes. Tad had suggested that they were enemies, but if so they concealed their hatred well. Lady Romanes seemed well satisfied with her baby's care, and Mistress Wysse was more pleasant than Jill had imagined she could be. They called each other "Cousin," gossiping and chatting about Archy as if they were real friends.

Jill, however, remained suspicious. She hadn't forgotten how rude Mistress Wysse had been when she took the salve, nor that she had been entertaining sinister Master

Rollo in the nursery. Jill had been disappointed when Tad, told of this incident, had been dismissive.

"I don't think that means much. I hadn't thought of Mistress Wysse in a conspirator's role," he had said in a rather lordly fashion. It seemed that if Tad had no ideas of his own, he wasn't going to let anyone else have them either.

On their way back from the nursery, Lady Romanes and Jill passed through the great chamber, the bedroom being got ready for Queen Mary, who was coming to spend the first six days of January at Gryffe. It was clear that a visit from the Queen was a great honour, however much Lord Romanes might grumble about the expense. There was to be a magnificent feast for the Queen's arrival, and in her room the angels on the newly painted ceiling glowed intensely among yellow suns, orange moons and silver stars. A new bed with a canopy and coverlet of violet silk was already in place.

"My lady, did you ever see the Queen?" asked Jill, as they paused to watch workmen on ladders hanging rich tapestries that had just arrived from France.

Lady Romanes shook her head.

"Never," she said. "Although she is little younger than I, Queen Mary left Scotland to live at the French court when she was five, and I had not left Drumspynie until I came here two years ago. My lord was in Edinburgh when she returned to Scotland last year, but—" Lady Romanes gave Jill one of her rare, impish smiles "—when I asked him what she was like, all he could tell me was that she stands taller than a man and is 'passing fair.' Passing fair, indeed! As if her beauty is not famous throughout the world, and half the lords of Scotland in love with her."

Though she sounded more amused than bitter, Jill decided it was time to change the subject.

"I'm sure the Queen will love sleeping in this beautiful room," she said, but Lady Romanes had lost interest.

"No doubt Her Majesty has slept in many fine rooms," she said indifferently as she moved towards the door.

As she followed, it struck Jill for the first time that Lady Romanes wasn't alone in her indifference. Excitement about this great event, now only a few days off, was generally muted. Some cleaning was going on, and Jill had heard from Bess and Lilly about preparations in the kitchen; a whole ox and a sheep were to be roasted, and already the pantry was bloody with the hung carcases of swans, partridges and geese. The cook was frantically planning syllabubs and almond tarts, and the cellar was full of choice French wines. But although everyone knew the Queen was coming, talk of her wasn't on everyone's lips.

Rather tactlessly, Jill mentioned this to Lady Romanes.

"It seems odd to me," she confided. "The Queen's coming to stay, for heaven's sake, and people don't seem very interested, do they?"

Lady Romanes opened the door of her room and looked down pensively at Jill in the wavering candlelight.

"I suppose that is because, at the moment, they are more interested in something else," she replied.

Jill hoped she only meant that they were absorbed in hunting and the relentless evening parties. In her heart, however, she was pretty sure that Lady Romanes was referring to the rumour that she was a witch. Fear and pity for the defenceless young woman swept over Jill, and fury with Tad, who had sworn to help her but was now intent only on amusing himself. Well, I'll stay with her and defend her, vowed Jill, winding up her courage. She little imagined that Lady Romanes had a very different plan. Later that same afternoon Jill learned what it was.

16

Quarrel

The sun was a crimson lantern on the horizon and night was falling frostily as the hunters came home. Jill had gone down to the courtyard to watch, because she loved to see the dogs and the horses, but had run upstairs to avoid seeing the carts that followed with their load of murdered deer and wild boar. She found Lady Romanes sitting at her table, sealing a letter with red wax and her gold signet ring. When she looked up Jill knew at once that trouble was brewing, but nothing could have prepared her for the shock to come.

"Jill, my love," said Lady Romanes, holding out her hand. "There is no easy way to tell you this, but I beg you to believe that it is for your own good."

"What is?" faltered Jill.

"I have decided to send you back to Drumspynie."

As these fateful words fell into her mind, Jill felt as if her feet had grown into the floor. The room was stuffy, but gooseflesh rippled coldly over her body.

"But why?" she wailed.

Lady Romanes reached out, took Jill's hand and drew her close. Jill stood stiffly, arching her back away from the encircling arm. Urgent words poured into her ear.

"Listen, Jill. I am in great danger, and I must ensure your safety. Dear heart, I cannot believe you have not heard what is being said. The whole house is humming with it. I am accused of spiriting away the miller's boy by witchcraft, and both my unfortunate face and my work of healing are held against me."

"No," cried Jill, but Lady Romanes' fingers firmly sealed her lips.

"I know where this vile rumour began, and I also know where it may end," she said hopelessly. Then she uttered words that made Jill's blood run cold. "Poor women have burned at the stake for less."

Jill began to sob wildly. She wanted to scream that it was all a mistake, that she wasn't really Jill Webster. She had only pressed "Enter" on the computer because she had wanted to be friends with Tad again, and if she was sent away to Drumspynie she might never find her way home. But she knew how incomprehensible such a tale would be to Lady Romanes, and despair silenced her. She heard the soft, throaty voice trying to explain.

"If I keep you here they may say that you are my apprentice, and you will be in danger too. Whatever

Rollo has in mind for me, I am determined he will not harm you. I have written to my father, asking him to send a servant he trusts to escort you north. If the weather holds, he should be here within four days. You will help to look after my Aunt Anne, but what matters is to have you under my father's protection. If this horror passes, I shall send for you again."

Another flash of memory not her own passed through Jill's mind, a bleak recollection of a querulous, bedridden woman whom only her niece Kate could soothe. Jill's heart sank even further.

"What about Tad?" she snivelled. "If I have to go, Tad ought to come with me."

Lady Romanes shook her head.

"My dear," she said, "you know I was only allowed to bring Tad here on condition that he became my lord's servant. He must stay here."

The tone was kind, but the words final, and it was their finality that steadied Jill. The resentment against her brother which had been simmering since Christmas Eve came suddenly to the boil. She blamed Tad bitterly—for luring her to this vile place with the promise of friendship, for his false assurance that he could outwit wicked Master Rollo, for his failure to do anything but swagger around and amuse himself. When Lady Romanes, complaining of headache, went into her bedroom to rest, Jill dried her eyes and went to look for Tad. She found him playing marbles with another boy outside the chamber of dais.

"I want to talk to you," said Jill so aggressively that Tad jerked up his head in astonishment.

His scruffy companion sat back on his heels, gave a rotten-toothed grin and said jeeringly, "Well, listen to my lady Webster!"

But when Tad saw Jill's sullen, tear-stained face he scooped up his marbles and dropped them into a leather pouch which hung on his belt.

"Later, Rab," he said, then to Jill, "Come with me." Jill followed him up some steps and along a dimly lit passage. At the end was a window with a wide stone sill. Her legs were trembling as she sank onto it. "You really shouldn't speak to me like that, you know," remarked Tad reproachfully as he perched beside her. "I'm Lord Romanes' page, and—"

"Oh, shut up," interrupted Jill furiously. "I don't care whose stupid page you are. All I care about is that after scaring me witless with your story about Rollo and Torkel, you're having a wonderful time and I'm having all the aggravation. Now Kate's heard the rumour about the miller's boy, and she's planning to send me away to Drumspynie to wait on that ghastly old Lady Anne. So what are you going to do about it, Big-boots, and when?"

She heard her voice rising hysterically and didn't care, but Tad glanced nervously along the passage. His face was chalk-white and his eyes distended in the pale light.

"Please, do try to be quiet," he whispered urgently. "Rollo's room is near here, and it won't help if he hears you squealing."

Jill hissed with annoyance, but the thought of the fearsome Rollo did make her lower her voice.

"I am not squealing," she growled. "I'm complaining. You were the one who said we had to protect Kate, and you were the one who was going to have a bright idea. But all you do is go hunting and show off with your silly lute—"

"Wait a minute—"

"No, you wait a minute," snarled Jill. "It was you who got me into this mess, and now I want to know how you're going to get me out of it, see?"

She was shaking more with temper now than with fear, and she could see Tad shaking too.

"Look," he said earnestly, "I'm sorry. I really am. I thought I had everything under control, but I'm stuck. I just can't think what to do next." There was a terrible pause; then he went on weakly, "I'm sure Kate doesn't mean it. She's just upset. It stands to reason."

"Oh, stop fudging," snapped Jill contemptuously. "Of course she means it. She's written to Lord Spynie asking him to send a servant to take me north." She couldn't help gulping as she added, "She says he could be here in four days."

"Four days?" Tad blew out his cheeks as if he had been granted a reprieve. "But that's ages. The way you've been carrying on, I thought you were leaving in the morning. I'm sure I'll have thought of a way to foil Rollo in four days. Maybe I could confront Torkel. I've got a knife—"

"And a big mouth," said Jill rudely as she got to her

feet. "Well, save yourself the trouble, Tad. You play your lute and I'll think of something myself."

She turned away from Tad's stricken face, stuck out her chin and strode away down the passage. A fierce glow of satisfaction warmed her, but it was doused next moment by the sad knowledge that once again she had fallen out with Tad.

17

The Wooden Horse

In the evening Jill told Lady Romanes that she had a sore stomach, and that the thought of venison and figgy pudding made her feel sick. Lady Romanes' remedy for a sore stomach was a spoonful of chamomile water; it had a bitter taste and didn't make Jill feel any better, probably because the pain wasn't really in her stomach. However, she was excused the night's revels in the great hall.

"I understand," said Lady Romanes wearily. "Would you like a basin of bread and milk? No? Then I think you should go to bed." As always, when she said good night, she made the sign of the cross on Jill's forehead with her thumb. "God guard you, Jill," she said, then added, "God guard us all."

Upstairs in the icy tower room Jill took off her shoes, stockings and dress. She folded the dress carefully and climbed onto her mattress in the shift that was both her petticoat and her nightgown. Shivering now with reaction as well as cold she drew her blanket around her, promising herself that as soon as she got warm she would have a good think. Obviously, since Tad had failed her, she would now have to fend for herself.

As the insulation of straw and wool heated her, however, Jill dozed, starting awake in the darkness with no idea of how long she had slept. She was relieved that there was no heavy breathing in the room; Lilly and Bess, who had constant colds and snored abominably, had not yet come up to bed.

Wide wake and feeling calmer, Jill curled up on her mattress and tried to recap what she knew. Rollo, already angry with Kate for marrying his brother, had gone wild when she had a little boy who would be Lord Romanes one day. He planned to punish her, and had bribed Torkel MacInnes to help him. Jill thought Torkel looked half-witted and wouldn't have trusted him to post a letter, but that was beside the point.

Rollo, apparently, was pleased with Torkel. He had said that Torkel had done well, which Jill supposed must mean that he had successfully spread the rumour that Lady Romanes was a witch who had magicked away the miller's lost child. Of course that was absurd, but Jill knew that she was now among people who believed seriously in witches and their evil power. Kate Romanes was in real danger.

But I'm going to save her, insisted Jill, feeling good

although she knew perfectly well that her first concern was to save herself. Only how should she proceed? The answer was simple, really. Don't hang around, like feeble Tad. Go and look for clues.

It was clear to Jill that looking to Master Rollo for clues would be pointless. She was so afraid that if she even glimpsed him she ran in the opposite direction. Even if she knew where his room was in this confusing stone maze, she'd never dare to go near it. Torkel was different. He slept next door with Tad and Rab and a gaggle of other boys.

Jill lay for a moment assessing the risk. She didn't know the time, but straining her ears she could hear distant music and laughter floating up through the court-yard from the windows of the great hall. Everyone would be there except for the sweating toilers in the ground floor kitchen. She would never have a better opportunity.

It took only a few moments for Jill to slip out of bed, run down to Lady Romanes' room in her shift and light a candle at the fire. Soon she was upstairs again in the boys' room, wrinkling her nose at the revolting smell of unwashed bodies and dirty bedding. She longed to open the little shutters in the lower window sash, but knew she mustn't leave any trace of her visit.

There were seven straw pallets lying higgledy-piggledy on the floor, but no other furniture at all. Jill knew which pallet was Tad's because he had left his spare doublet lying on it, but she groaned at the prospect of having to search another six. Still, there was no other way. Setting down the candle carefully on the floor, Jill threw back the fusty blanket on the bed nearest the door. She began to probe the mattress hastily with her fingers, afraid that at any minute the party might end and feet begin to clatter upstairs. By the time she reached the third bed her arms were covered with fresh flea bites and she was becoming frantic.

Then, quite suddenly, Jill found what she was looking for. On the side of the sack there was a slit, long enough for her to get her hand in among the straw. Groping feverishly, she pulled out three objects. The first was a greasy little canvas bag containing two groats and the tell-tale testoon. The second was a small, very sharp dagger. The third was a roughly carved wooden horse, about fifteen centimetres long, with nail-head eyes and a mane and tail of roughly shredded hessian.

Frowning in puzzlement, Jill held this unlikely object close to the candle. She saw that the letter *C* had been burned into its side with a hot wire, and also that its mane and tail were clogged with some kind of rough powder. Its faint smell reminded her of something, but what? It came to her suddenly—it was the porridge that everyone at Castle Gryffe ate for breakfast. It was also one of the storeroom smells. Oatmeal.

This wasn't at all what Jill had been hoping for when she put her hand into the mattress. She had imagined a letter from Rollo, incriminating both himself and Tor-kel—evidence which she could have taken straight to Lord Romanes. All the same, as Jill pushed her finds back among the straw and pulled up the blanket, she was very thoughtful.

Torkel, she reckoned, was about eighteen, and not at all the kind of person you could imagine keeping a toy for sentimental reasons. Besides, "Torkel" didn't begin with C. But if he wasn't the owner of the horse, who was? Jill was back in bed when a chilling theory began to form in her mind.

Jill recalled that when Tad had overheard Rollo and Torkel talking in the storeroom, Rollo had actually said that Torkel had done well *so far*. At the time she had been too alarmed to grasp the significance of this, and had barely thought of it since. But now, suddenly, it seemed vital to know what Torkel had "done well." She had been wrong to think that it was circulating the false rumour because—she now remembered—that had spread without him, "my lady being so witchlike." Jill shivered as the most likely explanation dawned on her.

Suppose, she thought, that Torkel, acting on Rollo's instructions, had waylaid the miller's boy and murdered him, stealing the toy which the child was carrying? If the little horse had come from the mill, that would explain its having oatmeal on its mane and tail. It was a horrific possibility, yet someone who kept a dagger in his bed would presumably be prepared to use it.

There were two problems, of course. One was how Torkel had disposed of the child's body, and the other was why he had kept the horse. Surely even a ninny would have got rid of it double quick. The only idea Jill came up with was that he might want to sell it. The testoon apart, Torkel was poor, and perhaps the toy would fetch a few pence at Perth market. Anyway, Jill felt she'd done as much thinking as she could for one night. Even the itching of her flea bites couldn't keep her awake any longer. She turned on her side and fell asleep.

18

Blind Man's Buff

"Lilly," ventured Jill, "may I ask you something?"

The three girls had dressed as usual by candlelight and Bess, who had to prepare the porridge for breakfast, had departed muttering downstairs. Lilly, shivering as she tried to push her coarse black hair under her grubby cap, wasn't in the mood for chat.

"Hurry up, then," she said snappishly. "I have work to do."

"I was wondering," Jill said. "Do you happen to know what the miller's boy was called, the one who was lost in the glen?"

As she spoke, she steeled herself for a suspicious response—"That's a funny question, surely? Why on earth do you want to know that?" But fortunately Lilly, who waited on Mistress Wysse at breakfast, had no time to lose.

"His name was Kit," she stated baldly, and next moment was clattering down the passage.

Jill couldn't help feeling disappointed as she pulled up the frilled collar of her shift over the straight neck of her dress, and pushed her feet into her shoes. She had quite made up her mind that the boy's name was Charles.

The morning dragged by without much to distinguish it from its forerunners, except that the queue of walking wounded at Lady Romanes' door had shrunk by more than half. Jill knew why, and that Lady Romanes knew why, but neither commented. Jill watched Lady Romanes pouring doses of medicine and cleaning up cuts and grazes. There was a trance-like expression in her eyes, as if she really couldn't believe what was happening to her. After the last wretched figure had hobbled away she shut her cupboard and told Jill to stir up the fire.

"Soon we shall have snow," she predicted, fingering the inflamed skin on her cheek. "Let us pray that my father's envoy is not delayed on the road from Drumspynie. I want you safely away from here before Master Rollo decides to stage the next act of his vile play."

Jill hoped that Lord Spynie's envoy would fall up to his neck in a snowdrift, but she wanted to comfort Lady Romanes. Turning with the poker in her hand, she said clearly, "Tad and I think that Master Rollo is jealous because Lord Romanes loves you so much." She was about to add, "If he does anything really awful my lord will thrash him again," but thought better of it. Instead she said, "I don't expect he'd dare to do anything really terrible," hoping she sounded more convinced than she felt.

Lady Romanes drew her chair close to the fire. The normal side of her face was white to the point of greyness.

"He will dare," she said. "Spreading rumour is only the beginning of Rollo's malice. He is planning some devilment which will ruin the Queen's visit, and for which I am to be blamed."

Again, fury with Tad bubbled up in Jill. This was what he had so lightly assured her wouldn't happen.

"But my lady," she began.

Lady Romanes silenced her.

"Last night in the chamber of dais," she said, "Rollo whispered in my ear that Her Majesty would have a very memorable visit. I knew by the way he smiled what 'memorable' meant."

Jill was ready to weep with vexation.

"I'm surprised he'd dare," she said. "I mean, if the Queen is upset, surely she may be angry with everyone?"

Lady Romanes shook her head.

"When the Queen was a little girl," she told Jill, "before she went to France, Master Rollo was a page at her court. He knows how to be charming when he chooses, and it is said the Queen doted on him. I think he knows her anger will not fall on him." She sighed and added bleakly, "If my lord had not loved me, he would never have risked ridicule by marrying me. For all the whispering that is going on, no one has yet dared to speak to him against me. Yet I dare say that when Rollo has done his worst, I shall find that my lord fears witchcraft as much as other men."

Jill went and put her arm round Lady Romanes. Just for a moment she was tempted to pour out what Tad had overheard, and tell her what she'd discovered last night in Torkel's bed. But she didn't, because she knew there was no point. Knowing what Tad had overheard would only add to Lady Romanes' anxiety, and Torkel's having a toy in his bed might be innocently explained. It might even, Jill thought acidly, make him seem quite a nice kind of person.

In the afternoon, however, as she sat on a stool winding silks round wooden bobbins for Lady Romanes' embroidery, Jill was more than ever convinced that the little horse had belonged to the miller's boy. The oatmeal clinging to its mane and tail was so very suggestive. Of course it was a setback to discover that the child's name began with *K*, but perhaps the horse had originally been made for someone else—his big brother, for instance. The thought of big brothers inevitably reminded Jill of Tad, and when she remembered Torkel's dagger she felt sick. She was furious with Tad, but she hated the idea that he was sharing a room with a murderer.

In the morning, Jill had been pleased with her own resourcefulness and elated by her discoveries. As darkness fell these feelings faded, and depression came down on her like a grey cloud. She had blamed Tad for not having ideas, but now she had to admit that she hadn't a clue what to do either. There seemed absolutely no way of discovering what Master Rollo had in mind, and it was hard to protect someone if you didn't know what you were protecting her from. So with only three days to go before she rode out from Gryffe on her way to Aberdeenshire, Jill too was reduced to waiting and hoping that something would turn up in time to avert a tragedy.

There was no way, Jill knew, that she could escape supper for a second night running. Like it or not, she had to sit through the noisy meal, disgusted by the slobbish behaviour of people who thought good table manners meant not spitting, and keeping your hat on so that head lice didn't fall into the food. As she picked fastidiously at a greasy goose leg, Jill watch Tad serving at the high board, but the sight of him upset her so much that she turned her attention to the other page, Torkel MacInnes.

To Jill's eye Torkel didn't really look like a murderer, but she reminded herself that appearances can deceive. The most striking thing about Torkel was that he seemed recently to have lost weight; his doublet hung loosely on his long body and his stockings were baggy and wrinkled at the ankles. Moreover, he didn't look a happy boy. His sallow face was lined with fatigue, and his dark eyes flickered nervously, particularly when he was in the vicinity of Master Rollo. Jill saw him spill sauce on the tablecloth, and try unsuccessfully to mop it up with his napkin. She couldn't hear Lord Romanes' rebuke, but observed the reddening of Torkel's large ears.

Even more than supper, Jill hated the long hours of wild dancing and games afterwards. The games were cruel, and usually ended with someone being humiliated or hurt. Even hiding in the stinking privy at the end of the servant's passage seemed preferable to taking part. Unfortunately, when Jill tried to sneak away during the table clearing, one of the older maids asked her to help fold the white linen cloths. By the time they had finished, it was too late. Lord and Lady Romanes, Master Rollo and Mistress Wysse came back from the chamber of dais, the minstrels struck up a galliard and Jill was dragged into the dance.

The Romanes family were only onlookers at the revels. Lady Romanes looked tired out, Lord Romanes could scarcely conceal his impatience and Mistress Wysse looked more like a glum frog than ever. As Jill jigged past the dais, she glanced fearfully at Master Rollo, pale and impassive under his black hat. She thought he was like a panther waiting silently to pounce, and was thankful that he was too high and mighty to join in. The idea of having to touch him in a ring dance scared her stiff.

Jill hoped that Lady Romanes would call her to sit at her feet or run an errand, but she didn't, and Jill had learned that it was wiser to take part than to show reluctance. When Bess had refused to play Snap-Dragon, a horrible game where you had to pick raisins out of a bowl of blazing brandy, she had been forced and had her hand burnt. Even when a game of Blind Man's Buff was proposed, and she was chosen as Blind Man, Jill didn't let

her distaste show. She resented its being Tad who tied the
blindfold tightly over her eyes, and hated the rough hands
that whirled her round until her head spun, but she kept
her mouth shut. A silence punctuated by sniggers followed as she began to grope around with outstretched
hands, desperate to grab someone and end her ordeal.

Jill's nerves were already on edge, and when other
players began to touch her she wanted to scream. One
tweaked her ruff, another kicked her ankle, a third prod-
ded her back. She snatched wildly at the air, provoking
unkind laughter. With difficulty Jill fought back panic
and paused to get her bearings. She heard a cough on her
left and made another snatch. This time she was lucky,
but as her right hand grasped a woollen sleeve something
was pushed into her left. Automatically her fingers closed
on it, and at the same moment her blindfold was torn off.
Blinking in the light Jill saw Tad grinning as he tied the
scarf over Torkel's lugubrious face.

As the game went on, Jill drew back and surreptitiously
explored her own palm. Her middle finger identified a
sheet of stiff paper, folded small. A message from Torkel,
she thought, feeling a cold paw at her heart. He had
allowed her to catch him so that he could press a note
into her hand. Terror clutched Jill—for why would Torkel MacInnes want to communicate with her, unless he
knew what she had been doing in his room last night?

Needing to be sure, Jill turned and ran out of the hall.
Her sweating body was jolted by the cold air as she slithered across the landing and dived through an archway to

the nearest candle sconce. With shaking fingers she unfolded the paper and read the scrawled words:

"Please don't be mad. We can work this out together. Come to the storeroom tonight when all are asleep. T."

Damn, thought Jill. Not Torkel, Tad. Biting her lip she leant against the wall, struggling with annoyance, self-ridicule and a huge sense of anticlimax. Very soon, however, all these feelings were submerged by a great wave of thankfulness. Pride had kept her going since last night, but it hadn't masked her pain. Now Jill admitted that more than anything in the world she wanted to be friends with Tad again.

19

A Walk on the Moor

By midnight Lilly and Bess were in bed and sleeping heavily. Jill was exhausted too, but determination kept her awake until noise in the castle had died away, and the only sound was the tread of the night watch on the battlements overhead. Presently she heard the cautious creak of Tad's door opening, so she got up and wrapped herself in her blanket. By the time she reached the moonlit storeroom Tad was already there.

"I'm glad you've come," he whispered, as Jill scrambled over the sacks to the corner where they'd sat before. "Will you be friends again?"

"Yes," said Jill readily, but added a warning. "That is, provided you stop swaggering and treating me as if I was a speck of dust. We're equal partners from now on. Agreed?"

"All right," said Tad. He arranged the end of his blanket over his feet and continued, "Listen then, partner. I
think it's time we started looking for clues."

Jill managed not to laugh, but it was a moment of
triumph and she enjoyed it.

"I already have," she said airily.

There was a little pause, then Tad said, "Um—you
have?"

"Yes," nodded Jill, and quickly told him what she had
found in Torkel's mattress and her theory about the little
horse. "I know it didn't have the right initial on," she
concluded, "but I'll swear it had oatmeal on its mane and
tail."

Provokingly the moon disappeared behind a cloud just
then, so Jill was denied the pleasure of Tad's thunder-
struck face. Still, his silence was eloquent.

Eventually he said hoarsely, "It did have the right initial. They called him Kit but his name was really Chris-
topher, and the horse was his, all right. I saw him playing
with it one day when I rode with my lord to do business
at the mill."

The last of Jill's triumph drained suddenly away.

"So that really was what Rollo meant when he said
Torkel had done well so far," she said soberly. "He'd
ordered Torkel to kill Kit, and Torkel had obeyed."

But Tad wasn't having this.

"No," he said vehemently. "I can't believe it. Torkel's
stupid and greedy, and it sounds as if he's up to his neck
in trouble. But there's no way he could kill anyone."

"How do you know?"

"He's too soft," said Tad bluntly. "He goes green if he sees a rabbit in a trap and he hates hunting. He practically gags at the kill."

"He has a knife," objected Jill.

"Everyone has a knife—"

"And Kit has disappeared, and his toy horse is in Torkel's mattress," persisted Jill. "What else do you think fits the facts?" Tad didn't answer, so she went on. "Time's running out, you know. Kate reckons Rollo's planning to do something awful while the Queen's here, and if she has her way I'll be halfway to Drumspynie by then. I think we should act now. Get the horse and take it to Lord Romanes. Suggest he question Torkel."

Jill thought this sounded positive, and was cross when Tad chuckled softly in the dark.

"I don't like to contradict you, partner," he said, "but you don't 'suggest' things to my lord if you want to keep your head on your shoulders. Besides, Torkel would say he'd found the horse in the glen and hadn't connected it with Kit—possible, if you know Torkel. He'd probably say he'd kept it to give to his little sister. And he'd know we were onto him, which is the last thing we want."

Jill saw that this was sensible. She stretched and yawned in the darkness.

"Look," Tad said. "We'd better get to bed now. I'm not going hunting tomorrow—my lord says I am to wait on my lady, so we should have a chance to talk during the day." He paused, then said perplexedly, "It does look as if Kit's been done away with, poor little kid. But why? I mean, it seems such a drastic way of setting Kate up, when Rollo could probably get the same effect by saying she'd been seen flying over Gryffe hill on a broomstick."

Jill knew that this was a very important question, and that almost certainly the answer would clarify the mystery of what Rollo Romanes was planning to do. She also had an infuriating feeling that sometime, somewhere, she had been within a whisker of knowing what the answer was. Only she couldn't remember. It was one o'clock in the morning, and she was too tired to think anymore. Within two minutes of crawling into bed she was asleep.

Lady Romanes had been right about the weather change, though morning hadn't brought the snowfall she feared and Jill longed for. The frost had thawed overnight and dawn revealed a soft, moist day. Mist like damp fur clung to the valley, and the hills were beige under a dingy sky.

"Since Tad is to attend us, I think we might walk on the moor today," said Lady Romanes to Jill. "Tad has been out hunting, but you and I have not been out of doors for days."

It was true, although Jill hadn't really noticed. The thick, firelit walls of Castle Gryffe seemed to have enclosed her, and she now had to concentrate really hard to remember that she was a visitor, not a resident of this outlandish place.

Lady Romanes' queue of patients had dwindled even

further. She didn't comment, but nor did she spend hours in her herb-scented pantry, preparing salves and tinctures which no one wanted. She had the resigned air of someone waiting for an inevitable disaster and merely looking for ways to pass the intervening time.

As for Jill, as she whiled away the morning playing dice with Tad, she couldn't rid herself of the conviction that she knew something important, but couldn't call it to mind. With the arrival of Lord Spynie's servant now only hours away, the thought threatened to drive her frantic. She was glad when, after their usual midday meal of cheese and oatcake, Lady Romanes sent her and Tad to fetch their cloaks.

A damp wind buffeted the three figures as they walked over the drawbridge and down the slope. Far away in the valley they could hear the hunting horns, but the only other sound was the incessant, echoing roar of the Clathy burn tumbling through the chasm beside the castle's west wall.

"Lord, how I hate that noise," sighed Lady Romanes fretfully. "Ever since I came to Gryffe it has been like the voice of doom to me, though I cannot tell why." Jill agreed that it was an awesome sound, but didn't say so. Silently she and Tad followed as Lady Romanes turned east, taking the sheep trail up onto the high moor. On the ridge above the castle she paused, holding the soft lining of her hood against her face to protect it from the wind. "We shall walk to the Middle Well," she said. "Run ahead if you like, but stay where I can see you."

At first it was a relief to run away from the track, bouncing on top of the springy heather and enjoying the boisterous wind. But it was impossible to ignore the melancholy figure walking behind them on the path.

"She looks so lonely," said Jill guiltily.

"I know. Let's go and keep her company," suggested Tad.

The Middle Well was the source of the Clathy burn, an icy spring gushing out of the peaty hillside. There the track divided. One branch dipped away into the next glen while the other, following the course of the burn, looped widely through the heather before descending again towards Gryffe.

"Unless you are feeling tired, Jill, we shall take the long way home," Lady Romanes said.

"Jill said she wasn't tired at all, so Tad handed Lady Romanes across the tiny log bridge and they set off again. Tad went in front and Jill walked hand in hand with Lady Romanes. The unsheltering loneliness of the moor troubled Jill; there wasn't an animal or a bird in sight, and no sound but the inane chatter of the burn. After the closeness of the castle it was quite disturbing, and she was glad when the path began to descend between the burn and the wood which clothed the western flank of Gryffe hill. Suddenly two things happened.

As Tad squealed, "Look!" A hare leapt the burn and ran into the heather, and Jill saw a cottage in a clearing to the right of the path. It was crudely built on a timber frame, with low dry-stone walls and a turf roof. There were no windows and the door was so low that even Jill couldn't have passed through without stooping.

"Who lives there?" she asked curiously.

"No one, in December," Lady Romanes told her. "The shepherd has taken the sheep down to the valley for the winter, and he will bring them up again in March. Do you remember Watt Hardie, our shepherd at Drumspynie, Jill? He used to make me wooden toys when I was a little girl."

Jill pretended that she remembered Watt, but as they walked down towards Castle Gryffe her mind was occupied with something else. Try as she might, she couldn't rid herself of the disquieting idea that someone had been watching them from the shepherd's cottage. She had—there was no other way of describing it—felt eyes.

Glancing over her shoulder, Jill couldn't decide whether it was a wisp of smoke or a rag of mist she saw wavering over the dark roof—but of one thing she had no doubt at all. When they got to the stepping-stones over the burn above the castle, and Tad was helping Lady Romanes across, Jill's eye was caught by a furtive movement on the hill. A moment later she saw Torkel Mac-Innes creeping furtively down the path.

20

The Man in Black

Jill was afraid that she wouldn't have the opportunity to talk to Tad alone, but later in the afternoon, when she went to visit the nursery, Lady Romanes left the children by the fire in her room.

"Since you have only a short while together," she said kindly, "I shall leave you to enjoy it." She looked anxiously at Jill as she added, "If the weather holds, we can expect my father's messenger by dusk tomorrow. You will leave at first light the following morning."

"But that's the day the Queen is arriving," objected Jill. "Please, my lady, let me stay long enough to see the Queen."

The answer was straightforward.

"Certainly not. Tomorrow will be your last day at

Gryffe, but you will both have a holiday. I have arranged it with my lord."

Jill hadn't expected a reprieve, and didn't waste time sulking. The moment the door had closed behind Lady Romanes she swept aside the cards she and Tad were playing with and sat back on her heels. Breathlessly she told him what she had seen on the hillside.

"I can't be absolutely sure there was someone in the cottage," she concluded, "but I'm sure about Torkel. And if he wasn't visiting the hut, what was he doing up on the hill?"

Tad was alert, his eyes round gleams of excitement.

"I think you're onto something," he said. "This morning Torkel asked Lord Romanes to excuse him from hunting so that he could go and visit his sister, who was ill. My lord said that if he had a groat for every time he'd heard that story he'd be able to afford the Queen's entertainment, but he said yes. Torkel's no use at the hunt anyway. Now, his sister lives down in the village during the winter, but the fishy thing is that she keeps house for Torkel's father, who is Lord Romanes' shepherd. In the summer months they live in that cottage by the wood."

Jill took in this information, then said slowly, "Well, well. So what do we do now?"

She tried to sound cool, but her heart was pumping hard. Tad glanced up at the grey, rain-streaked window and shook his head.

"Right now, nothing," he said regretfully. "It's lashing rain and almost dark, and besides, I have to attend my lord in half an hour. But since Kate has arranged for us to have a holiday tomorrow—"

"We'll go and see what's what," Jill finished for him. "I wonder what we'll find?"

"Something more interesting than Torkel's sister, I'll bet," said Tad darkly, which Jill took to mean that he really hadn't a clue.

All the same, suddenly optimism was stirring in Jill. She was still afraid that the day after tomorrow she would be riding pillion on a horse heading north, but as she took a candle and went upstairs to tidy herself, she felt more positive than she had since this adventure began. Although the niggling anxiety about what she wasn't re-membering remained, she hoped that if the shepherd's cottage revealed a clue to Rollo's intentions, her remem-bering wouldn't matter. At the same time, Jill suspected that her courage would soon be severely tested. Upstairs something happened which underlined the probability.

As Jill went along the passage to her room, a dreadful smell floated around her. It was a combination of stale body odours, dirty bedding and the vile reek which gusted from the insanitary privy nearby. Castle Gryffe was full of bad smells, and Jill noticed them less than she had, but as she pushed open her bedroom door this one was so bad that she felt sick.

Lilly and Bess objected strongly to having the window open—understandably, since the temperature in the room was barely above freezing. But, they were down in the kitchen, and it seemed to Jill that it would be better to shiver a little than to be asphyxiated. She put down her candle and climbed onto the windowsill. As she fiddled with the catch on the little shutters a movement caught her eye. Curiously she peered down through the wet upper sash into the courtyard below.

On the far side, sheltering under the archway and just visible in the dying light were two figures. Jill recognised instantly the gangling figure of Torkel MacInnes, and the equally unmistakable outline of Master Rollo, the man in black. She watched them in earnest conversation and then saw Master Rollo nod and clap Torkel approvingly on the shoulder. Torkel disappeared through the arch and Rollo paused for an instant, pulling up his dark cloak over his head.

I've been here before, thought Jill, but then forgot, because as she watched the huge, bat-like creature loping across the yard to the door, she felt a terror so overwhelming that she almost fell off the sill. She closed her eyes and held onto the window frame until the blackness in her mind dissolved; when she dared to look again the courtyard was empty. But Jill had had a warning of evil so strong that for the first and only time in her life she wished someone dead.

21

Torkel's Story

There was no hunting next day. With only thirty-six hours remaining before the Queen's arrival, the leisurely preparations of the previous week were suddenly suffused by a new urgency. Lord Romanes strode to and fro bellowing orders and everyone was involved, from Master Rollo down to the smallest kennel boy. Servants scurried to and fro with brooms and polishing rags. Sweet herbs were strewn over the newly laid rushes and the sparse furniture rubbed up with beeswax. In the kitchen the cook was close to nervous collapse.

Although Lord Romanes had officially given them a holiday, Tad and Jill were drawn into the stir. Tad spent most of the morning replenishing the drooping decorations in the hall and helping to hang a new tapestry panel as a "cloth of state" behind the chair on the dais that the

Queen would occupy. Jill helped Lady Romanes to lift gowns from the clothes chest in her bedroom and lay them on the bed. It was clear that Lady Romanes had no interest in what she would wear, but Jill tried hard to encourage her.

"This dark green velvet is beautiful, my lady. It would look so well with your rose taffeta petticoat, don't you think?" When this question evoked no reply she persevered. "On the other hand, your russet brocade might be more suitable, with your cloth-of-gold headdress and a lawn veil. I always think you look beautiful in that gown."

Lady Romanes must have known that this was meant sincerely. Instead of raising her eyebrows and making a bitter remark at her own expense, she put an affectionate arm round Jill.

"My dear child," she said. "How badly I shall miss you. Pray God you will return to me one day."

Jill stood by the bed, thoughtfully fingering velvet and stiffly embroidered brocade. Eventually she said, "My lady, why don't you come to Drumspynie too? If your father will protect me, surely he'd be even more willing to protect you?"

Lady Romanes smiled ruefully and shook her head.

"I cannot say it has never crossed my mind," she admitted. "But how could I, Jill? I should have to leave my baby, and everyone would think I had run because I was guilty." She paused, then added, "If I am executed as a witch, my father's revenge on the Romanes will be terrible. But a wife belongs to her husband, not to her father."

"I see," said Jill, although she really found the idea of one person being the property of another impossible to understand.

With one thing and another, it was midday before Tad and Jill were free to put on their cloaks and escape from the castle. It had snowed overnight, but with the indecisiveness that marks the Scottish weather, morning had brought a quick thaw and a blue sky. Swollen by melted snow, the Clathy burn was swirling around the stepping-stones and roaring even more loudly than usual as it toppled into the gorge.

"We must stay under the trees," Tad said, "and approach the cottage from behind. At least Torkel's out of the way. He's cleaning my lord's boots, which will keep him busy for a bit."

"What about Rollo?" asked Jill nervously, recalling her terror on the windowsill.

"In charge of finding accommodation for the Queen's household," said Tad with a faint grin. "Since it means turning us all out of our beds, he's greatly enjoying it."

"What a pig," said Jill.

Creeping under the eaves of the wood, Jill found the going hard. Branches of bramble caught at her skirt and before long the hem was wet and dirty. At length, however, Castle Gryffe dropped out of sight and she saw the shepherd's cottage squatting like a large brown animal among the trees. This time there was no doubt. A feeble drift of smoke wafted from a hole in the roof.

"Keep down low," instructed Tad, "and be ready to drop if we see anyone. We'd better crawl the last bit."

They didn't see anyone, but were cautious anyway, creeping and worming over the leaf-mouldy ground until they reached the rear wall. Jill had been wondering how they were going to see into a windowless house, but there wasn't a problem. The walls were built without mortar and there were quite wide chinks between the stones. Peering into the firelit interior, the children had to suppress gasps of excitement.

On a flat stone in the middle of the single room a peat fire burned crimson, illuminating the cracked, smoke-blackened walls. Beside it on a stool crouched an unkempt girl of about fifteen; she had long black hair, and the firelight shone on a face like enough Torkel's to identify her as his sister. The girl was stirring a steaming iron pan with a stick.

No other furniture was visible, but the watchers' attention was alerted by a movement on a pile of straw and animal skins tumbled against the gable wall. It was hard to see properly, and at first Jill thought there was a dog. But when Tad started violently and whispered, "My God, it's Kit," she saw that there was indeed a small human being lying in the straw, tied by a rope to an iron ring on the wall.

"What shall we do?" mouthed Jill, but before Tad had time to answer there was a warning crack as someone behind them trod on a twig. Whipping round in alarm, the children saw Torkel MacInnes advancing towards them through the trees. Tad had miscalculated how long it took to clean a pair of boots.

It was a dreadful moment. Jill shrank back gasping against the wall while Tad groped under his cloak for the small knife he carried in his belt. There was a ghastly pause while they stared at Torkel and he stared at them. What happened next was unexpected.

Suddenly Torkel crumpled. His sallow face went grey, his eyes stared and his thin body began to shake uncontrollably. Jill thought he was going to faint. Her own fear evaporated as Tad strode forward, took Torkel by the arm and made him sit down with his back to a tree trunk.

"Take it easy, Tork," he advised, and Jill too approached, looking at the shuddering figure with solemn eyes. She and Tad sat down on a fallen trunk and waited for Torkel to control himself. It took a few moments, but eventually he raised a hopeless face from his knees.

"I—that is, I mean," he stuttered, then stopped, licking his dry lips.

Tad said, "Why don't you tell us everything?"

"Yes, do," urged Jill, surprising herself. "Perhaps we can help."

Torkel shook his head.

"No one can help," he said, but he told them anyway:

"When Master Rollo was here in September, just after Master Archy was born, he caught me stealing a gold ring from Lord Romanes' chest in the chamber of dais. Of course if he had told my lord I might have been killed, though more likely I'd have been thrashed and set to herd pigs, because my lord values my father. But Master Rollo said he wouldn't tell, provided I promised to return the favour when he asked me."

"And he asked you to kidnap Kit," breathed Jill, horrified.

"No. He ordered me to kill Kit," corrected Torkel. "Although he pretended he'd just arrived from France ten days ago, Master Rollo had really been in the district for weeks. One day he jumped out on me when I was going down the glen and said it was time for me to repay my debt. He told me he planned to get rid of Master Archy, and make sure that Lady Kate had no more children to take away what was rightly his."

Tad groaned and Jill cried out in horror, but Torkel ignored them. Licking his lips again, he pressed on. "Of course me doing all the dirty work was the main part of the plan. I was told to grab a child, any child, then kill him and bury his body in the peat bog on the high moor. Then I was to start a rumour that Lady Kate had spirited the child away by witchcraft. Later on, when Master Archy disappeared, people would say, 'She did it once, and now she's done it again.' "

Tad was looking crestfallen, but Jill was furious with herself. She had suddenly remembered what had been eluding her for two days. On Christmas Eve, Tad had played his lute and sung the plaintive words,

Lully lulla, thou little tiny child,
By, by, lully lullay.
O sisters too, how may we do
For to preserve this day
This poor youngling . . .

and Lady Romanes had wept. Jill recalled sitting on the dais, wondering whether her tears were for the miller's boy, or for her own little son. What a fool I was, she thought. Surely I might have seen how the first crime was the clue to the second. But Torkel hadn't finished.

"I didn't want to do it," he was half sobbing. "I like Lady Kate. But Master Rollo said if I didn't, he'd tell Lord Romanes about the ring and kill my little sister. So when I saw Kit in the glen I captured him—only I couldn't murder him."

"So you brought him to the cottage," said Tad.

Torkel nodded.

"I tied him up," he said. "I took his wooden horse and told him he'd get it back if he didn't make a noise. I was going to leave him, but I realised he'd freeze to death. So I got my sister Tib to come up and look after him. My plan was to hold him till tonight, when I'm supposed to drown Master Archy in the glen pool. Instead I'd bring the baby up here, and—"

"Tonight?" screamed Jill.

Again Torkel's large head nodded.

"Master Rollo said it must be tonight," he said, "to provide an entertainment for the Queen tomorrow."

Now it was Jill who was shaking violently, but Tad said, "Tork, I think you had better tell us what's going to happen tonight."

"All right," Torkel agreed.

The plan was simple, and devilish. Mistress Wysse, who had been bribed by Rollo with the promise that she would take charge of the household again after Lady Romanes' execution, was to excuse herself from supper in the great hall. As soon as the meal was over, Torkel was to slip away and go to the nursery. There Mistress Wysse would hand over Archy.

"I knew that woman was a crook," burst out Jill indignantly, but Tad said, "Sh-sh. Go on, Tork."

Torkel explained that he was to take the baby out through the unguarded west gate, which opened onto a strip of grassland where the burn deepened as it ran towards the chasm. A heavy stone and rope were already hidden under the wall, and soon a defenceless infant would be hurtling to his death in the glen pool.

"Mistress Wysse is to give me time to do the deed," Torkel went on, "then she is to run to the hall, screaming that the child has been spirited from his cradle as she sat by the fire. Of course there will be an uproar and Master Rollo, never having been out of my lord's sight, will reluctantly whisper his suspicion into his brother's ear." Torkel sniffed and wiped his nose on his cuff. "Only it won't be like that," he said. "I couldn't kill a baby, for God's sake. I'll bring him up here, then I'm off into the heather with Tib. I don't know why all this has happened to me."

There was a self-righteous, self-pitying whine in his voice which infuriated Jill. He wasn't exactly an innocent victim, after all.

"Listen you," she growled. "You won't bring Archy up here because none of this wickedness is going to happen, see? We're going straight back to Gryffe now to tell Lord Romanes."

This seemed to Jill such an obvious course of action that she was annoyed and surprised when Tad contradicted her. He had been looking quite dazed, but suddenly he spoke with authority.

"No, Jill," he said. "Don't you see? Rollo has worked this out so cleverly that there isn't a scrap of evidence against him. He'd accuse us of lying, and Lord Romanes would believe him. Torkel would be hanged for kidnapping Kit and we'd be whipped for daring to speak against our lord's brother. After a while Rollo would try again, and we'd be powerless to help Kate and Archy."

Jill saw that this was true. She gritted her teeth in frustration.

"So?" she said, and was amazed, in the waning light, to see Tad looking positively cocky. He had the air of someone who had fallen off a horse but was now firmly back in the saddle.

"Here's what we'll do," he said. "Jill, you must play truant from supper and come up here to the cottage.

Tork, you must follow your own plan and bring Archy up here. Jill will look after him and Kit while you take Tib home to the village by Middle Well. What you do then is up to you, but I advise you to confess to Lord Romanes and ask for mercy.

"I'll stay behind until Mistress Wysse does her staggering into the hall act, then when Master Rollo starts whispering to my lord I'll interrupt and say I know where Kit and Archy are. If Rollo contradicts me—and I bet he will—he'll give himself away. I'll bring Lord Romanes up to the cottage, and he'll find Kit and Archy safe and sound."

"It will be pitch dark," objected Jill, but Tad had an answer to that too.

"It's full moon," he crowed, as if he had never heard of clouds.

Jill sighed. Tad's confidence seemed to sap hers, and it bothered her that he seemed to be snatching back the power to plan and make things happen. But she went along with him because, at the moment, she didn't know what else to do.

22

Websters' Leap

Jill sat on Tib's stool by the fire, with Archibald Adair Romanes whimpering sleepily in her lap. Little Kit, dirty and dishevelled but remarkably calm, played with his wooden horse in the straw. Occasionally he yawned and asked, "Shall I be going home soon, Jill?"

"Very soon, Kit," Jill assured him. "Tad will bring Lord Romanes, and he will take you home."

She was actually beginning to believe it, because everything had gone according to plan, so far. Even the moon, riding brilliantly in a clear, frosty sky, seemed eager to please. Jill had felt bad about skipping supper without permission, but knew that Lady Romanes wouldn't worry; she would simply think that Jill was hiding from the dark young man in Lord Spynie's livery who had ridden into the courtyard at dusk. It had been quite easy to slip out of the west gate, cross the stepping-stones and follow her small moonshadow up the track between the racing burn and the silent wood. Jill had been nervous, but determination had made her brave.

Tib, warned by Torkel, had given her a cautious welcome, and the two girls had crouched by the fire until Torkel arrived. He was carrying Archy in a blanket and had Kit's toy horse in his belt.

"We're off now," he had said, dumping Lord Romanes' heir unceremoniously on Jill's knee. "Come on, Tib."

Jill hadn't even had time to say goodbye before she heard their footsteps receding up the path towards Middle Well. Left alone with the two young children, Jill prayed fervently that Tad and Lord Romanes would come soon. She didn't know when Archy had last been fed, and there seemed to be nothing edible in the cottage except some thin left-over porridge, still steaming in a pan over the fire.

After a while, though, Archy fell asleep, and the silence was broken only by an owl hooting in the wood and the rustling of the straw where Kit played. Jill couldn't help imagining the scene at the castle, and her heart ached for poor Lady Romanes. Her anguish would be terrible when her enemy rushed into the hall, screaming that her baby had disappeared.

Lully lulla, thou little tiny child,
By, by, lully lullay . . .

Surely by now, Jill thought, Tad must have challenged the unspeakable Rollo, and Rollo, taken by surprise, would have shouted, "This boy is a liar! I know—"

"What do you know?" Tad would then cry, and when Lord Romanes saw fear and uncertainty in his brother's eyes, the plot would begin to crumble. But haven't they had time enough? Jill wondered. She felt as if she had been in this draughty cottage for hours.

"Shall I be going home soon, Jill?" Kit asked again.

"Yes, soon." The words were scarcely out of Jill's mouth when she heard footsteps thudding up the track. Her heart leapt and she began to say, "Here they come, Kit. Didn't I tell you?"

But before she could finish the sheepskin which covered the doorway was sent swinging as Tad hurtled violently into the room. He was panting loudly and his eyes were wide with alarm.

"Disaster," he gasped. "Everything's gone wrong." He was in pain from a stitch in his side, but continued bitterly, "When I tried to tell Lord Romanes where Archy was he wouldn't listen. He's ridden off like a madman to search the village. Rollo heard, though. I thought I'd got clear, but when I was at the stepping-stones I looked back and saw him on the drawbridge. He's on his way up. We must run—"

But it was too late. In a moment of utter terror the children saw the sheepskin torn down, and a black figure slide snake-like under the narrow lintel. As it reared upright Jill rose from the stool and Kit ran to her side.

Slowly the children drew back, huddling on the far side of the fire. Rollo Romanes stood with his hands on his hips, looking at them with his unnaturally glittering blue eyes.

"How convenient. Four rats in one trap," he sneered. "Now I can give myself the pleasure of slitting your throat, Master Webster, but I think I shall slay these other vermin first. A fitting punishment for kidnapping the heir of Gryffe, I think, not to mention meddling in my affairs. A pity that Master Archibald will die in the struggle you put up. My brother will be most distressed."

As he put his hand on the hilt of his dagger, Kit set up a thin wail of fear, but Tad acted. With a speed that astonished Jill he leapt forward, whipped up the pan of scalding porridge and threw it in Rollo Romanes' face. As Rollo screamed and raised clawing hands, Tad head-butted him in the stomach and set him flying onto his back in the straw. Rollo's velvet hat fell off, and there was a dull thud as his cropped head hit the wall.

"Follow me," yelled Tad, and a moment later the children were crashing into the wood behind the house. A moment of fierce triumph was spoiled by the howling and cursing they could hear behind. Their enemy was hurt but conscious, and he still had the use of his legs.

As the noise died away, however, an unnerving silence took its place. It was dark under the trees, the bare branches intersecting like veins against the starry sky. Presently Tad paused and whispered, "Listen. We must go down through the wood and try to come out just above the stepping-stones. Then we'll have to run for it. Jill, give me Archy. My arms are stronger than yours. Kit, hang onto Jill's hand, and don't make a sound. And cheer up—Rollo can't know where we are or he'd be here by now."

Jill didn't find this entirely reassuring. She handed over Archy, who was now awake but miraculously silent, and took Kit's trembling little hand in hers. His need steadied her, and she gave his fingers a friendly squeeze.

"Cheer up, Kit. You'll soon be home now," she said.

The next quarter of an hour was harrowing, punctuated by terrible moments when the undergrowth rustled or a twig snapped sharply underfoot. But there was no sound of pursuit, and as she stumbled after Tad through the wood Jill felt a glimmering hope that Rollo had been too badly disabled to leave the cottage. Presently Tad veered left and the wood's edge appeared, arches of pale light between the pillars of the trees.

"When we get to the path," instructed Tad softly, "wait till I say 'Go', then dash for the stepping-stones. Once we're over, run like hell."

For a moment or two it really seemed possible, and Jill's optimism increased. Only when the children got close enough to the path to see the stepping-stones, and the haven of Castle Gryffe suspended on the night sky beyond, her hope was sharply snuffed out. Standing at the stepping-stones with his dagger drawn was Rollo Romanes. He had simply walked down the path and was now waiting for them to abandon the shelter of the wood.

"Damnation," cursed Tad under his breath. "Back, then, into the trees."

They retreated and stood in a miserable huddle a few metres from the path. They were all cold and Kit was shivering violently in his thin tunic, though fortunately too shocked to cry out. Archy lay as quietly in Tad's arms as if he knew that his life too depended on silence. Jill was in despair, but Tad refused to give up.

"Hold on, Jill," he whispered. "We still have a chance."

"Do we?"

"Yes. If we go on down through the wood beyond the stepping-stones, we can cross further downstream."

Jill thought this was silly, and said so.

"The water's far too deep," she pointed out. "We'd all be drowned, or swept over the waterfall."

"I know that," hissed Tad, suddenly impatient. "I don't mean we should try to wade. We'll sprint from the end of the wood, jump the chasm and make for the west gate. Even if Rollo sees us, we'll be over before he has time to run down the bank. What d'you say?"

For the first time, self-control completely deserted Jill. A vision of the hungrily sucking black hole between the rocks swam before her eyes and she began to gabble wildly.

"Tad, don't make me jump the chasm. Please don't. I'll slip and fall down the waterfall. Let's go back and see if we can make it round by Middle Well. Please—"

"No." Tad's tone was relentless. "These little ones

would die of cold on the moor. Come on, Jill. Do it for Archy and Kit. Do it for Kate."

Put like that, it didn't seem to Jill that she had a choice. Her stomach heaved, but she put her arm round Kit's thin shoulders and began creeping further down through the trees.

The wood ended abruptly some twenty metres from the cliff edge. As the children emerged they could hear the eager roaring of the waterfall above the splashing of the burn. The moon shone on a patch of exposed hillside between the trees and the chasm; looking uphill, Jill could see Rollo still standing motionless at the stepping-stones. Across the burn the west gate stood open, and she was aware of torchlight in the garden beyond. Tad offered some last words of advice.

"I'll go first with Archy," he said, "then you and Kit together, Jill. The gap isn't wide, and if we keep our heads and don't look down, we'll make it all right. Can you jump, Kit?"

"Yes," said Kit. It was the first time he had uttered a word since he left the cottage. "I mustn't drop my horse, though."

Despite the gravity of their plight, Tad and Jill couldn't help smiling at this.

"Right then," said Tad. "Now!"

He shot out into the open and Jill followed, hand in hand with Kit. Immediately there was a shout of rage from above, and Rollo Romanes began to lope down the bank towards them. Tad reached the chasm and leapt,

clutching Archy to his chest. Jill hesitated briefly, but
when she saw the distance closing between her and the
murderous Rollo she shouted, "Jump, Kit!"

Bunching up her skirt with her free hand, she soared
from one black stone and landed on another; strong hands
grabbed her and Kit and hauled them to safety under the
castle wall. In the light of torches Jill saw Lady Romanes
with the young man from Drumspynie and Torkel, who
had gone bravely back to Gryffe to tell his tale.

Jill was heaving a huge sigh of relief when she heard a
thin, piercing scream rising above the noise of the water.
Whirling round, she saw Rollo Romanes poised on the
far side of the chasm. For a split second she glimpsed his
blistered face with lips drawn back over yellow teeth, a
hideous mask of hatred and fear. The stone which had
borne the children's lighter weight was rocking under his;
his arms flailed helplessly as it split from the bank and he
went head first into the gorge. His howls were drowned
by the clamour of the torrent as he plunged to his death
below. Lady Romanes made the sign of the cross as Jill
collapsed on the grass at her feet.

Afterwards, Jill remembered being carried through the
garden by Lord Spynie's servant, and being undressed
and put to bed by Lady Romanes.

"How is Archy? Is he all right?" she asked anxiously.

"Archy is well. Sleep, my dear, and we shall talk in the
morning," said Lady Romanes.

But when Jill felt the thumb printing the cross on her
forehead, somehow she knew that it was for the last time.

Lady Romanes had wrapped extra blankets round her, and warmth seeped through Jill's exhausted body. She thought she couldn't forget the scene of horror she had just witnessed, yet it was quite another image that appeared behind her eyelids as she drifted towards sleep.

What she saw was her own room at home in Ealing, and Tad sitting at her computer desk by a window full of summer leaves. Strangely, he had his eyes closed, and his right hand poised over the on/off switch. As he pressed it, Jill went out like a light.

23

An Unexpected Arrival

Next morning Jill knew she was back in the twentieth century before she opened her eyes. The mattress was firm, the pillow and duvet soft and clean-smelling. When she did open her eyes she saw Tad's familiar bookshelves and computer, and the summer sun slanting across the striped rug on the floor.

Suddenly remembering, Jill put her hand under the pillow and pulled out the postcard portrait. Lady Romanes' dark, inscrutable eyes looked into hers, and she was overwhelmed by a mystery she thought she could never understand. As she got out of bed and switched off the computer, something told Jill that its magic would never work for her again. With the rescuing of Kit and Archy, her part in the Romanes' story was played out.

"Morning. Sleep well?" asked her father casually as she arrived in the kitchen for breakfast.

Such a simple, everyday question, yet Jill didn't know how to answer it. She had been away for nine long days, enduring hardship with people who had lived more than four hundred years ago, yet to him it had apparently been no longer than a night in bed. She poured cornflakes into a bowl and sat down by the window, staring out over the dark green treetops.

After Mr Weaver had gone into the office, Jill went downstairs and wandered through the cold rooms she had known firelit and teeming with uncouth life. Lady Romanes' room and her bedroom were easily found, as were the great hall and the room Jill had seen prepared for the visit of the Queen. What had happened, she wondered, when Queen Mary arrived to discover that her childhood favourite had died earlier while intent on murdering his own nephew? Rollo had told Lady Romanes that the Queen would have a memorable visit, and memorable it must have been. Jill knew that nobody in their right mind would choose to live in such uncomfortable, half-savage times, yet she would have liked to see the Queen and had a sense of being snatched out of a great adventure. She felt flat, and Castle Gryffe as a "tourist attraction" seemed insufferably tame.

Looking for Archy's nursery, Jill found that the entrance to the passage had been bricked up. When she went out of doors she realised that this was because a great part of sixteenth-century Gryffe had been demolished. The little chapel where Katherine Romanes had knelt to pray had been attached to the east wall. Now it stood apart, a forlorn little enclosure with grass growing between the stones on the floor.

Sadly Jill went down the steps into the garden where bees droned in the honeysuckle, out onto the grassy strip beyond the west gate. The wood opposite was now a straggle of scrubby trees, and the chasm the children had leapt was overhung with knotgrass and golden saxifrage. But the water still swirled ominously between the rocks, and Jill remembered with cold revulsion the ghastly moonlit face of Rollo Romanes in the second before he plummeted into the gorge.

Sickened by memory, Jill ran back into the sunlit garden. As she went up the steps into the courtyard, however, something interesting came back to her. In the film that had started this weird affair, Tad had mentioned that the chasm was known as Websters' Leap and the pool below as Rollo's Well. It must have been a famous story, she thought, if these names were still remembered after so long.

In the afternoon, since it wasn't a day when the castle was open, Jill worked in the garden that Kate Romanes had planned. First she weeded among the mint and chamomile, then she clipped the dead heads of the white Burnet rose. She thought about Kate, but the gentle spirit was absent, and Jill's depression deepened. The rest of the summer stretched ahead, a desert of boredom. At half-past four she went wearily indoors.

It was unusual to hear Mr Weaver on the telephone. Even when he left the office door open because it was hot, the thick walls absorbed his voice. So when, from the floor below, Jill heard him hollering blue murder, she ran upstairs. She didn't have to hear both sides of the conversation to grasp what was going on.

"Run away? You stupid little twerp! Does Mum know? You left her a note? That was good of you. And where the hell are you now? *Glasgow airport?* I don't believe this. Too right, I'll come and fetch you. Go and ring your mother, then stay put till I get there."

Mr Weaver slammed down the phone and catapulted through the door, almost squashing Jill against the wall. His face was scarlet with rage.

"Dad," began Jill, but he wouldn't listen.

"Well," he barked, as if it was all Jill's fault, "your brother has excelled himself. He doesn't like your mother's cooking, or her boyfriend, or her cat. He's at Glasgow airport, and I'm on my way to kill him."

"May I come too?" asked Jill eagerly.

"No, you may not. What I have to say to that young man is best said in private. Goodbye."

He grabbed his car keys from a hook behind the door and ran downstairs. Jill heard the engine start up and the car accelerate out of the courtyard. Wild with excitement she ran into her room and bounced on the bed. Tad was at Glasgow airport. In two hours he would be home.

Jill's euphoria lasted for fully five minutes before a sudden thought killed it. Oh lord, she groaned. What a fool I am. For of course the Tad who was waiting at the airport wasn't Tad Webster, with whom she had shared friendship and adventure in the days of the Romanes. He was her brother Tad Weaver, who hated her so much that he hadn't spoken to her once at York, and had put up rude notices in Edinburgh forbidding her to touch his things. This would be no happy reunion of friends, only another sullen stand-off between two spitting cats.

Jill spent the next two hours prowling tensely around the flat, lifting things and putting them down, looking at the clock. She had tummy pains and couldn't settle to anything. Half-past five passed, then half-past six. At ten to seven she began to worry in case Dad had had an accident. It was just on the hour when she heard, through the open sitting-room window, the sound of the car coming up the hill.

Jill dashed along the passage to her bedroom and jumped up on the windowsill. Far below she saw the car bump over the cobbles and stop at the foot of the tower. Mr Weaver got out, slammed the door and strode indoors. There was a pause, then the door on the passenger side opened and Tad got out. He was wearing blue jeans and a white T-shirt, and his bright head shone in the mellow evening sun. Jill watched him open the boot and take out his waxed jacket, a nylon rucksack and his battered lute case. Her heart was knocking on her ribs and she wished there was somewhere she could hide.

Then something amazing happened. Tad stood for a moment with his belongings at his feet, then slowly he tipped back his head and looked straight up at the window where Jill was. She saw him grin, wink and wiggle his fingers in a comical greeting. Jill leapt off the windowsill and went downstairs like the wind.

24

Tad Weaver

The evening had been hilarious, the more so because Dad wasn't in the mood to appreciate jokes. At half-past seven he had gone down to Gryffe village to buy fish and chips, leaving Tad and Jill to lay the table. They hadn't spoken much, but when Tad had made remarks like, "The old guy's freaking out," and "I bet Ms Chancellor's going bananas," Jill had giggled merrily. When Mr Weaver had thrown the fish and chips onto plates and they were all three sitting at the table, she'd scarcely dared to look at Tad. Every time he got up to fetch something he rolled his eyes wildly behind Dad's back and pulled the corners of his mouth down with his fingers. Jill thought she would choke on swallowed laughter.

After supper Mr Weaver had banged off to the office to

telephone his ex-wife, while Tad did the washing-up and Jill went to have her bath.

"We'll talk later," promised Tad, "when Sourface has gone to bed."

Jill thought Tad was very laid-back about his father's displeasure until she remembered that Dad's fury was like a tornado. If you could keep your head down, it passed over.

Tad was to sleep on the sofa in the sitting-room, but when Jill was in bed he appeared in his dressing-gown with two mugs of coffee. He gave one to Jill and sat down on the end of the bed. They looked at each other in silence for quite a while. It was Jill who spoke first.

"Why did you really come back?" she asked. "I don't believe it was just because Mum's on a healthy eating crusade."

Tad smiled faintly, but his face quickly became serious.

"No," he agreed. "After Rollo crashed into the gorge last night, I saw you lying in a faint on the grass. Suddenly I was appalled by what I'd made you go through, and when I switched the computer off I swore that must be the end of the adventure. I knew I had to see you to apologise and explain, and that there was no way I could explain to Mum why I had to leave. So when she went to work this morning I packed up and left. I caught a train from South Ealing to Heathrow and got on an afternoon flight. Fortunately I hadn't spent any of my holiday pocket money."

Jill wasn't surprised by the bit about the computer. She

believed that she'd been drawn into the past by Tad's computer, so it made sense that he had been drawn in by hers. She remembered visualising him switching off the computer in Ealing, just at the moment when she too realised that the adventure was over. What she couldn't understand was why Tad was blaming himself.

"You needn't apologise," she assured him. "You didn't make me go through it. We were just living in dangerous times."

Tad drew up his legs and settled back against the wall. After a pause he said, "There's more to it than that, Jill. You see, it was my story."

Jill hadn't a clue what he was talking about.

"Sorry," she said. "What story do you mean?"

Tad looked uncomfortable.

"You asked me in the storeroom on Christmas Eve how I'd got there," he said, "and I didn't know how to explain. But I'll try now. Just listen, will you?"

Jill nodded dumbly.

"OK," said Tad. "I'd better start at the beginning. When I came to live at Gryffe I thought everything was magic—the castle, the countryside, the wildlife. Only one thing spoiled it. I like company, and I didn't have anyone my own age to share it with. I really wanted you, but you'd fallen out with me—"

"Hang on," interrupted Jill indignantly. "It was your own fault—choosing to stay with Dad instead of Mum, then going off to Edinburgh, grinning all over your face."

Tad looked startled.

"Oh, come on," he said. "Fair's fair. Why should Dad have been left on his own, without one of us to keep him company? As for me wanting to go to Edinburgh, that was only because I was due to move up to Woodley High School. Those kids they called the Daws Road mafia went there, and I was terrified of them. Surely you knew that."

"No," pouted Jill, but then honesty made her add, "I don't suppose I ever gave you the chance to tell me. Sorry."

"So am I," replied Tad, but with these mysteries solved he went on with his story. "Anyway, I really missed you, and I used to imagine that you were here and we were having fun together. In March Dad and I made a film, and I dressed up in my costume for the school play. I pretended that you were here too, and that we lived at Gryffe in the time of Mary, Queen of Scots. That was the beginning for me, I suppose."

And for me, thought Jill, remembering vividly her first night at Gryffe.

"Go on then," she urged.

Tad gulped some coffee.

"During the winter, Dad borrowed some books about Gryffe from the library," he said. "In one of them I read the legend of Websters' Leap. It said that Lord Romanes had a psychopathic younger brother called Rollo, who was so jealous of his nephew that he wanted to kill him. He stole the baby and took him to the wood, but the child was rescued by a servant called Webster who jumped the chasm to get him safely home. When Rollo tried to catch up he met a sticky end—hence the name "Rollo's Well."

The word *legend* bothered Jill.

"Doesn't that mean that it wasn't really true?" she asked.

"It means that it might have been true," said Tad, avoiding her eye. "Anyway, I didn't think a lot about it until Easter, when Dad and I went up north to visit Drumspynie. "Drumspynie's amazing—when Dad's stopped spitting out tacks I'll ask him to take us both there. You can see all sorts of things that belonged to the Adairs and the Romanes. There's a famous painting of Kate and Archibald Romanes, and a tiny silver cup and spoon that Mary, Queen of Scots gave to the baby when she visited Gryffe in 1563. But the thing that fascinated me most was a book."

"What kind of book?"

"Lord Romanes' account book. It was in a glass case, open at a page showing his wages bill for Midsummer 1562. Wait—I took a copy and I have it here somewhere."

Tad got up and padded over to a cupboard by the window. After some searching he took a sheet of paper from a file and brought it to Jill. There were two columns, one with the Romanes' servants' names and one with their wages. Jill wasn't interested in the wages, but there were names that fascinated her as much as they had Tad.

. . . Master George Seton, armourer
Mistress Flora Wysse, nurse
Master Torkel MacInnes, manservant
Master Thaddeus Webster, page
Mistress Jill Webster, my lady's maid . . .

"It was Dad who pointed out the coincidence of the names," said Tad. "He said that 'Webster' was the old Scots name for 'Weaver'. So they really did have the same names as us."

Jill couldn't help feeling smug.

"So I was right," she said. "There really were two people called Tad and Jill Webster. They looked exactly like us, and when we went back into the past everyone mistook us for them. They were our historical twins, Tad." She was eager to tell him how she had known Jill Webster's past and sometimes shared her thoughts, but there was a wary look in Tad's eyes that stopped her. "Well?" she said uncertainly.

Tad shook his head.

"That's a clever idea," he admitted. "But the truth's even stranger."

Jill was only slightly mollified by the word *clever*. She frowned, but managed to say, "OK. What, then?" civilly enough.

Tad took up his tale.

"When I got back from Drumspynie," he said, "I couldn't get Kate Romanes and the Websters out of my

mind, or the story about Websters' Leap. I read everything I could lay my hands on about the sixteenth century. Dad gave me a lute for my birthday and I taught
myself to play the Coventry carol—another story about
babies being hunted by a villain. Do you remember?

> *"Herod the king,*
> *In his raging,*
> *Charged he hath this day*
> *His men of might,*
> *In his own sight,*
> *All young children to slay.*

"It fitted in, somehow. I knew I was going to be bored
stiff in Ealing, with Mum at work and that silly squit
Justin prancing about the house, so I hit on the idea of
writing a novel about Gryffe four hundred years ago. I
asked Mum if I could use your computer, and—"

"Wait a minute!" screeched Jill, bouncing up from the
pillow as the word *novel* struck her brain. That was what
Amanda Cameron's story had been, a hundred and
twenty pages about people who had never existed and
events that had never happened. "Are you telling me you
made the whole thing up?" she demanded. "That I was
just a character in your book?" She almost choked as she
added bitterly, "That nothing that happened to me was
really true?"

25

Fact and Fiction

Tad glanced fearfully at Jill's scarlet face and put his head in his hands.

"Yes," he said. "No. Not exactly."

"Yes, no, not exactly?" repeated Jill incredulously. "What dumb kind of answer is that?"

There were tears of anger and betrayal in her eyes, because she felt she'd been made a complete fool of. Tad looked up imploringly.

"Look," he said. "I didn't intend to trick you. I had no idea that it would be anything but a holiday pastime. What happened amazed me just as much as you, honestly."

"Big deal," muttered Jill, but she couldn't help being disarmed by Tad's frankness. He was obviously speaking the truth. "Well, tell me," she added grudgingly.

Tad relaxed a little.

"It was a historical novel," he said, "so a lot of things were true. There was a problem with the language, because in the sixteenth century people here spoke a kind of Scots I couldn't begin to understand, but since it was a story I made them speak English. But all the characters in the story really lived, except for Kit, Tib, Bess and Lilly. I invented them because the story seemed to need them. Kate Romanes really was a herbalist, and she had a terrible facial deformity due to an accident at birth. That was in the Drumspynie guide book, with a story about how Hans Eworth painted her looking beautiful because she warned him that if he painted her truthfully Lord Romanes would kick him downstairs. There's a portrait of Rollo at Drumspynie too, all in black and looking evil.

"I found the account of the 1562 Christmas celebrations at Gryffe in one of Dad's library books, and everyone really was getting ready for a visit from the Queen on New Year's Day. As for the legend of Websters' Leap—we do know there was a servant called Webster, so it may have been true, although I admit there's no proof it happened at Christmas. Anyway, I had so many ideas banging around in my head that I just couldn't resist making a story out of them." He laughed softly and added, "Except that, as it turned out, a lot of the story was invented by you."

Jill, who had been calming down, was suddenly irritated again.

"Don't try to butter me up," she snapped. "I thought

Jill Webster was putting thoughts into my mind, but now it turns out that you were. So how can you say that I invented anything?"

"Because you did," insisted Tad. "Don't you remember?" He finished his coffee and put the mug on the floor. "When I started writing it was wonderful. The story just kept coming into my head. I wrote about Kate Adair adopting two children called Webster, really you and me, and bringing them to Gryffe. I wrote about Rollo having a tantrum when Archibald was born, and plotting to get his own back on Kate by accusing her of witchcraft."

"You made that up?" asked Jill, who was surprised to feel deep relief when Tad nodded.

"Afraid so," he admitted. "I had great fun writing about my adventures as Lord Romanes' page, riding and hunting and learning to fence, but it wasn't until I was writing about something quite simple—going into Lady Romanes' room with a jug of wine—that I found out something extraordinary. If I shut my eyes and imagined really hard, I could get right inside my story. Everything else melted away, and I was at Gryffe with you as my friend. After that I seemed to go to and fro between Ealing and Gryffe all day long, and I was pretty sure that what was happening to me was happening to you too."

Jill nodded thoughtfully.

"The first time I got into the past was the day you served wine to Lady Romanes," she said. "You waved to me. But I didn't invent anything, Tad. Obviously my mind was picking up signals from yours—like when I mentioned Drumspynie to Kate without ever having heard of the place—but I thought what you were inventing was really true."

She didn't say this reproachfully, because it was now ceasing to matter, but she really thought Tad was wrong. She heard him chuckle.

"Oh, I certainly meant to do all the inventing," he said. "When I started the story I intended to be the cool, resourceful hero who would outwit Rollo and save Kate and Archy. You were supposed to be my cute little sister, thrilled to bits to have such a clever big brother."

"Fat chance," hooted Jill derisively.

She knew that this was a spot-on description of her old relationship with Tad, but she'd grown up a lot since then.

"Quite," grinned Tad. "You may have been a character in my book, but you didn't half live a life of your own. My big problem was that after I'd made my fine speech in Kate's room about how we couldn't let the dirty rat Rollo destroy her, I got completely stuck. I couldn't think what should happen next, and I got so sick of you whining that I decided to give you a little trip to Drumspynie while I waited for inspiration. But you had other ideas, hadn't you?"

"Too right," exploded Jill, but she was beginning to understand.

"After that, you were the one who put thoughts into my head," said Tad. "I don't know what would have happened if you hadn't started to push the story along. It was your idea to search Torkel's bed and find the little horse, and your idea to find Kit in the shepherd's cottage. And it was you who worked out that Mistress Wysse had to be in the conspiracy. I'd just thought of her as a nasty woman."

"So I helped with the plot," said Jill, feeling both surprised and gratified. "I didn't realise."

Tad grimaced.

"Maybe I should have let you finish it," he said. "If I had agreed to go straight to Lord Romanes after Torkel confessed in the wood, it would have saved you a very nasty experience. But I was determined that the story would end with me bravely jumping the chasm with Archy, like in the legend. That was why I sort of grabbed it back and set it up so that it would finish the way I wanted. Sorry."

Jill remembered how she had been aware that this was happening, but hadn't understood why, at the time. Now she said magnanimously, "You needn't be sorry. Yours was a far more exciting ending, though I'm thankful it was just a story. I loved Lady Romanes, and I'd hate to know that such vile things really happened to her."

Tad nodded.

"I liked her a lot too," he agreed. "It must have been terrible to be so disfigured, but she was a brave, clever woman who trusted God and made a good life for herself. She was a scholar and a famous healer, and Lord Romanes called her 'my most perfect jewel.' She had six children and lived to a ripe old age."

"I'm glad I know that," Jill said. Reassured, she let Lady Romanes resume her real place in history and turned her mind to the other Tad and Jill. Now that she knew their lives had only been imagined by Tad and herself, she realised that she knew nothing about them at all. "I wonder what the Websters were really like," she said.

Tad shrugged his shoulders.

"Who can tell?" he said. "Poor, unimportant people don't leave much trace. But whoever they were, they could have had worse employers."

Jill reckoned that this was true. Jill Webster, "my lady's maid," would have been kindly treated by Kate Romanes. Jill was becoming sleepy, but one thing still bothered her.

"Tad," she said. "Remember you said you got into the story by shutting your eyes and imagining really hard? I had to put a disc in the computer and press 'Enter' before I could get in. I wonder why?"

Tad rose and picked up the coffee mugs.

"I can't be sure," he said, "but I think that was probably just a coincidence. What happened really had nothing to do with computers. It had to do with you and me needing to find a way of getting together again and making up our quarrel. It all happened in our minds, and minds are more amazing than computers, after all."

Yes, thought Jill. That would explain why neither Dad nor the old lady had seen her on the video film, and why Dad and Lady Romanes hadn't seemed to miss her when she went from one time into another. It would always be mysterious, but Tad's explanation was as close to the truth as she would ever get. She curled up and pulled the duvet up to her ears.

"Pity we didn't see the Queen, though," she sighed regretfully.

Tad laughed as he opened the door.

"Actually," he said, "I scribbled that chapter this afternoon while I was waiting for my flight at Heathrow. I'll read it to you in the morning, if you like."

"Is it fact or fiction?" mumbled Jill.

"Both," Tad replied.

26

The Coming of the Queen

Next morning Tad and Jill sat on a bench in Kate Romanes' garden, under the golden August sun. Bees droned among the flowers, and the next bad weather was still only a purple streak on the horizon.

"Ready?" asked Tad, opening a blue folder.

Jill nodded and shut her eyes. As Tad began to read, the people she had known appeared to her for the last time.

"Lord Romanes was deeply distressed by his brother's death, because he had looked after him since he was a little boy. When he realised the extent of Rollo's wickedness, however, he was thankful not to have the unpleasant task of punishing him. Lady Romanes would never forget the terrible sight she had seen at the chasm, but she was comforted by the rescue of her baby and her own escape from Rollo's false accusation of witchcraft. Tad and Jill were each rewarded with a purse of gold, and since he had been the victim of blackmail Torkel was lightly punished. His testoon was confiscated and he became a kennel boy. Mistress Flora Wysse made off into the heather during the night, and was never heard of again."

"That's not very likely," objected Jill, but Tad said amiably, "Shut up. This is my chapter:

"Next morning, they all had to put their recent bad experiences behind them, for nothing must be allowed to spoil the arrival of the Queen. Jill was called to lace Lady Romanes into her russet brocade gown, and put on her clean ruff and gold embroidered cap. Tad, looking very smart in his best tunic and with a feather in his cap, helped Lord Romanes fasten his sword-belt and handed him his gloves.

"The Queen had spent the night at Dunfermline, and was due at Gryffe before nightfall. As the afternoon wore on, excitement mounted. Colourful banners were hung in the courtyard and fresh rushes strewn where the Queen would dismount. Wonderful smells of roasting meat, quite unlike Ms Rose Chancellor's macrobiotic gunge, floated from the kitchen, and everyone was looking forward to supper."

"When do we get to the facts?" giggled Jill.

"Now," Tad said.

"As the sun went down like a crimson ball on the western sky, a trumpet brayed from the battlements of Gryffe. It was the signal that the Queen's procession had been sighted in the valley, and immediately the Romanes and their household took up their positions for the royal welcome. They had to wait longer than they expected.

"Ages seemed to pass and Lord Romanes began to fidget, wondering whether the trumpeter had made a mistake. At last, the reason for the procession's slow progress became clear. Into the courtyard lumbered three huge wagons pulled by sweating oxen and loaded with trunks, boxes and bulging sacks. It was a miracle they had made it up the hill. Lord Romanes stared at the Queen's luggage and turned white.

" 'Her Majesty means to stay with us forever,' he groaned, and his wife couldn't hold back a smile.

" 'We have food enough in the house if she does,' she replied.

"Next came the Queen's retinue, snooty gentlemen in velvet cloaks and vain ladies who would have looked prettier if their noses hadn't glowed like rubies in the cold. They dismounted and stood around the yard, 'twittering like sparrows,' as Lady Romanes later said. Their pages ran to seize the horses' bridles, and Lord Romanes' chief groom showed them to the stable.

"A further twenty minutes passed. Everyone was stiff with cold. But at last a fanfare of trumpets rang out from the castle wall as Queen Mary, escorted by twelve armed bodyguards, rode in at the gate. Looking down from a window, Tad and Jill Webster saw a tall, stately lady in dark velvet, her head covered by a veil flowing from a pearl-embroidered cap, dismount at the tower door. Lord Romanes bowed, then knelt to kiss her hand. He rose, turned and drew forward his wife. When Lady Romanes curtseyed, the Queen raised her up, smiled and kissed her on the cheek."

"Is that true?" asked Jill longingly.

"Yes," said Tad. "It's all in a letter Kate wrote to her father the day after the Queen went away. They got on really well, and the Queen thought Archy was a peach."

"Great," said Jill, but then added sadly, "It was a shame, what happened to the Queen later on. Having her head chopped off, I mean."

"True," agreed Tad, "but that's another story."

As Tad closed his folder, Mr Weaver ran down the steps into the garden. He came and sat between Jill and Tad on the bench, tipping back his head to enjoy the sun. The tornado had passed over.

"Since you two seem to have sorted yourselves out," he said, "I was wondering if you'd fancy a trip to Drum-spynie next weekend? You'll hardly believe this, Tad, but since she came here Jill's got to be as keen on the past as you are."

"Imagine," murmured Tad.